# MISTAKEN AMBUSH!

Quickly, before the ambusher had time to recover, Longarm tried to throw a punch. The two were much too close together. There was neither space nor leverage for such a blow, and his punch landed ineffectually on the muscle pad of the ambusher's shoulder.

Longarm tried again, this time with a viciously chopping elbow that caught the ambusher on the left temple. Longarm felt his opponent's head snap back and the body beneath his suddenly go limp.

Before he had time to rise, or even to turn, he was jumped from behind.

Longarm twisted and kicked out at his attacker.

He heard a yelp of pain. And a familiar voice. He stopped fighting and let the hard hands of George and the stage driver pull him away from the limp body of the would-be ambusher.

"Longarm?" The stage driver gave Longarm a look of undisguised disgust. "I never woulda took you for a rapist, damn you."

# DON'T MISS THESE
## ALL-ACTION WESTERN SERIES
### FROM THE BERKLEY PUBLISHING GROUP

**THE GUNSMITH by J. R. Roberts**
   Clint Adams was a legend among lawmen, outlaws, and ladies. They called him . . . the Gunsmith.

**LONGARM by Tabor Evans**
   The popular long-running series about U.S. Deputy Marshal Long—his life, his loves, his fight for justice.

**SLOCUM by Jake Logan**
   Today's longest-running action Western. John Slocum rides a deadly trail of hot blood and cold steel.

**McMASTERS by Lee Morgan**
   The blazing new series from the creators of Longarm. When McMasters shoots, he shoots to kill. To his enemies, he is the most dangerous man they have ever known.

→ TABOR EVANS →

# LONGARM

## AND THE DEADLY THAW

J

JOVE BOOKS, NEW YORK

LONGARM AND THE DEADLY THAW

A Jove Book/published by arrangement with
the author

PRINTING HISTORY
Jove edition/June 1995

ISBN: 0-515-11634-3

A JOVE BOOK®
Jove Books are published by The Berkley Publishing Group,
200 Madison Avenue, New York, New York 10016.
JOVE and the "J" design
are trademarks belonging to Jove Publications, Inc.

PRINTED IN THE UNITED STATES OF AMERICA

10  9  8  7  6  5  4  3  2  1

AND THE
DEADLY THAW

# Chapter 1

Longarm came awake with an alarming sense that he was drowning. In a tub of warm water, or . . . Comprehension came half a second behind wakefulness, and he began to smile. He reached down to his crotch. His searching fingers encountered not his own wiry thatch of pubic hair but a wispy puff of curling softness. It was bright gold in color, he knew without bothering to open his eyes.

He gently stroked the back of Dame Edith's patrician head while the lady's lips and talented tongue continued to stroke him. All in all not a bad way to awaken, he decided as he stretched his lean frame. But carefully, so as not to take anything of interest out of the lady's reach.

And lady she was, at least on the far side of the big water. Edy Dunn had been a showgirl in a small London theater. Dame Edith Fullerton-Welpole was a celebrated society hostess. Also a damned good lay, as Longarm could attest.

As for Lord Matthew, all Longarm knew about him was that he was seventy-four, had rotten teeth and breath like a walrus—how Edith knew what a walrus's breath smelled like Longarm did not pretend to know and did not want to ask—and was at the moment engaged in a boringly long hunt somewhere in the wilds of Montana. When Edith

1

spoke of the place Longarm was convinced that upper Montana must surely be somewhere on the other side of darkest Africa. Or possibly more distant than that.

And while Lord Matthew was away, his poor darling had languished in solitude here in Denver.

Until, that is, she'd caught Longarm's eye—or more aptly, he'd caught hers—and an invitation had been issued.

And how could a gentleman possibly refuse a lady's gracious invitation? It would have been churlish in the extreme. And so, no cad he, Longarm now lay in the lady's high canopy bed and arched his back to accommodate her somewhat muffled demand for "more . . . deeper . . . yes."

He was engaged in a not altogether unpleasant debate over whether to come inside her mouth this time, as Dame Edith herself seemed to prefer, or to tug her astride so she could spear herself on top of him and make it that way.

The debate was set aside at least for the moment by a discreet tapping at the bedroom door.

"Shit," Dame Edith said loudly.

"Sorry t' int'rupt, m'lady, but there's a most persistent gentleman 'ere t' see yer, um, visitor," a woman's voice said. "Beggin' yer pardon."

Edith gave Longarm a look of clear annoyance, but all he could do was shrug. "I didn't tell anybody where I'd be."

"I should jolly well hope not."

"Reckon I'd best go chase off whoever's there, all right?"

"Make it quickly, luv. I shouldn't want all my juices to dry up whilst I wait for you. Now would I?"

"No, we sure couldn't have that," he agreed. He slipped out of the bed and into his trousers and shirt, pulling his black cavalry boots on without the formality of socks. He did not bother with his vest or coat. But before moving to the door he did belt on the big Colt .44 in its cross-draw holster. He would as soon go to the door naked as go without the double-action Colt. No, actually he would *rather*

2

go naked than without the gun. Embarrassment is *so* much easier to get over than death, after all.

"This way, sir," the homely little maid told him, a touch of scarlet putting color into her cheeks when she got a glance at the gentleman who had been entertaining her lady.

It was a reaction that Longarm got from women gratifyingly often, and one he certainly did not mind even though he could not honestly understand it.

The face he saw when he shaved each morning was, in his own opinion, more rugged than classically handsome, with sun-wrinkled features and piercing brown eyes. He had a strong jaw and a huge, sweeping brown mustache, dark brown hair, and a healthily tanned complexion. He stood something over six feet in height, and had broad shoulders that tapered to a horseman's narrow waist and flat belly.

The little maid—it was Longarm's observation that women whose power depends upon their beauty generally surround themselves with plain servants and companions—bobbed her head and dropped into a sort of curtsy as she pointed to the door leading into this top-floor suite from the hallway beyond. "If you'd be needin' anything, sir . . ."

"I'm fine, thank you."

The maid backed away far enough to give the pretense of not being able to overhear, and Longarm peeped out to see who was calling.

He frowned.

"Henry! What the hell are you doing here? It's Sunday morning, for cryin' out loud, and I'm not on duty again till tomorrow."

"Wrong," Henry declared with no remorse whatsoever. The slightly built fellow, whose meek appearance belied a firm resolve whenever push came to shove, was secretary, confidant, and aide to William "Billy" Vail, United States marshal for the Denver District, United States Justice Department. Custis Long, known to his friends and to a good

3

many enemies as Longarm, was Billy Vail's top deputy. A deputy who at the moment was supposed to be off duty and was not pleased with this interruption.

"Go away, Henry. I'll see you an' the boss come morning."

"Sorry, Custis. He needs you."

"On a Sunday morning?"

Henry grinned.

"What's so funny?"

"It's the middle of Sunday afternoon, for one thing. And you haven't been down to take a meal, nor had one sent in, since yesterday noon. What I think is that the marshal is doing you a favor by calling you back to work. You need the rest."

"Someday I'm gonna ask you how the hell you find out all the things you do. You know that?"

"Who knows. Someday maybe I'll answer you if you do ask. So anyway . . . Can I tell him you're on your way?"

"Yeah, hell, you know you can. Tell him I'm fifteen . . ." Longarm glanced behind him in the direction of the bedroom he just left. "Tell him I'm half an hour behind you. Okay?"

"Don't be any longer than that, Custis. You have a train to catch this evening."

Before Longarm had a chance to ask for an explanation, Henry was ambling away down the hall.

Longarm stepped back and let the door swing shut, then reached for a cheroot and matches.

A train to catch on a Sunday evening? He found that his curiosity was getting the better of him.

He felt his chin. Coarse grit and sandpaper. But if he didn't take time to shave he figured he could make it to the office not more than ten minutes behind Henry.

Dame Edith would just have to wait.

# Chapter 2

Longarm paused on the landing before going the rest of the way down into the hotel lobby. He adjusted the string tie at his throat and tugged at the bottom of his vest. At this time of year he preferred a fairly heavy calfskin vest for its extra warmth and laid his usual tweed coat aside in favor of a heavy sheepskin-lined ranch coat. As always, though, the familiar gold watch chain dangled loose across his belly. That chain and its attachments had been of great service on more than one occasion, for at one end of it there was the expected railroad-quality Ingersoll key-wind pocket watch, but at the other, instead of a decorative fob, there was a far more utilitarian item, a small brass-framed .44-caliber derringer.

Satisfied that his appearance was as good as he was going to get after such a hasty departure—made all the more swift by Edith's fury when he told her he had to leave—Longarm clamped his cheroot between his teeth at a jaunty angle and made his way on down into the lobby.

He needn't have been concerned about his appearance, it turned out. Apart from the hotel staff there were only two guests in the place, and they were engrossed in reading their newspapers. Longarm nodded a pleasant good day to the clerk behind the counter and strode toward the wide entryway where a doorman in a gold-trimmed red coat was waiting. Before Longarm came near, the doorman snapped to attention as crisply as a West Pointer could have managed, and a whole lot more smartly than any private soldier Longarm had ever seen. The fellow fairly jumped at his chance to open the door. Not for Longarm, as it happened, but for a young, handsome, and quite obviously wealthy swell who was heading in from outdoors.

The newcomer came breezing in amid a flurry of swirling snowflakes. It hadn't looked like snow the last time Longarm poked his head outside, but then February weather is never predictable in the High Plains country. And Denver is situated to catch the worst of the plains storms and the tail end of the bitter mountain storms as well.

The swell was greeted with so much enthusiasm that Longarm would have found it damned well embarrassing, but this young gent took it all in stride as if it were his due.

He was, Longarm noted in passing, tall and built with all the tough resilience of a sword blade. His hair was blond and curly, giving him a soft and almost feminine look. Until one noticed his eyes. The fellow, for all his wealth and pampering, had the cool and confident look of a gambler. And a damned successful one at that. Longarm suspected this was not a man he would want to face across a gaming table. Nor a dueling ground either, unless it was Longarm who was given the choice of weapons. This looked like a very competent gent indeed.

Longarm gave the fellow a polite nod and went by him.

"Welcome back, Lord Matthew," the desk clerk enthused loudly.

Lord Matthew indeed! The elderly impotent of the walrus breath and the cuckold's horns?

Longarm slowed and paused by the door to take another look at the man in whose bed he would surely have been caught if not for Henry's recent intrusion.

"I thought the gent was off shooting buffalo. Or something," he muttered to the doorman.

"Lord Matthew? Oh, no, sir. Lord Matthew don't do much shooting. Though I hear he has his hired hunters to collect trophies for him to take back to his estates. Kind of an odd sort, he is. Or so they say. Me, all I know is that he spends free and easy. Catch his eye and there's sure to be one of them English sovereigns, gold ones they are, to put in your pocket right soon. Oh, he's a spender, that one is. But . . . different from the way an American would be. Thinks his shit don't stink just because he's a lord." The doorman shrugged. "What the hell, is what I say." The shrug gave way to a grin. "Just so long as he keeps on handing out them gold coins, right?"

"Yeah, I'm sure," Longarm said. But as he looked back at Lord Matthew, who now was heading up the stairs toward his gorgeous wife, Longarm couldn't help wondering if Dame Edith had been playing a deliberate and malicious game today.

Was that why the lady was so pissed off when Longarm told her he was leaving? Had she been expecting her husband's return today? If so, Billy Vail had gone and ruined it all by taking Longarm away before all the players were assembled.

Too bad.

Longarm nodded a cheery good-bye to the doorman—no point in insulting the fellow with a dime tip when it was gold sovereigns he had in mine—and went outside.

Once the hotel doors were securely closed behind him he began laughing out loud. The silly bitch and her walrus-breath lord of a husband indeed.

Longarm was going to have to do something nice for Henry, he decided. Something by way of a thank-you.

Then, turning his coat collar up against the bitter wind and the snow the wind carried with it, he hunched his shoulders and made his way in the direction of Colfax Avenue and the chill mausoleum that he knew the empty Federal Building would be on a dreary Sunday afternoon in February.

7

• • •

"I'm sorry to drag you down here like this," Billy Vail said.

"Don't be. I didn't mind in the least," Longarm told him cheerfully. And, as it turned out, honestly.

Billy gave him a frankly skeptical look, then decided to accept the statement at face value. "The reason I didn't want to wait until tomorrow, Longarm, is that we have a tip that Cy Berman has been spotted in a town called Talking Water up in Wyoming Territory."

"Never heard of it," Longarm said.

"That's understandable. The people who live there hadn't heard of it until last year or so."

"Gold camp?"

"Uh-huh. Shirttail sort of place, I suspect. If things hold true to form it should last another season or two and then fade away. Not that you have to care about that, of course. What that does affect, however, is the status of law in that part of the territory. Talking Water has no town marshal, or at least not that I can ascertain. The town, not incorporated, is in Ross County. The sheriff of Ross County is a gent named Andrew Thomas Dillmore. Do you know him?"

"No, should I?"

"Not particularly, but I was hoping."

"Go ahead an' spit it out, Billy. Our boy Cyrus Berman has been spotted in this half-baked gold camp and there is local law available but Berman ain't in custody. So what's the story? Why do I have to rush up there an' put the cuffs on him when this . . . what'd you say his name is?"

"Dillmore, Andrew Thomas."

"Right. Sheriff Dillmore. Why hasn't Dillmore put Berman in the pokey where the sonuvabitch belongs?" Cy Berman, as every deputy U.S. marshal west of St. Louis damned well knew, was high on the want list of the Attorney General and of every swinging dick beneath him. It was bad enough that Berman made a fat living by robbing

8

mail cars. What was worse was that the bastard had shot down three postal inspectors and a U.S. deputy marshal, a man named Squires from Seattle who Longarm never met but nonetheless felt for. Berman was quick to shoot and had neither mercy nor remorse. There wasn't a federal officer anywhere who didn't want this one put away.

And now to have some local shit-for-brains refuse to wrap him up? Longarm was already getting pissed just thinking about it.

"I've sent two wires to the man since this tip came in," Billy said. "And the tipster, by the way, said he had already tried to get Dillmore to arrest Berman but was refused. I received one reply from Dillmore. All it said was, and I quote to you the full text of the message: 'No cause to arrest.'"

"No cause?" Longarm came halfway out of his chair in protest. "The sonuvabitch has—"

"Dammit, Long, you don't have to convince me. Tell it to this Dillmore person."

"Damn right I'll tell him. I'll put him in iron as quick as Berman if that's what it takes, Billy. You should know that right up front. If that sonuvabitch Berman resists he'll get a .44 in his teeth as a persuader. And if Dillmore wants to take sides it's his tough luck."

"Do whatever you have to, Long. If there is any heat from the territorial authorities in Cheyenne, the United States attorney here is prepared to back you up. We've already discussed that. Which is not to say that you are being given license to run wild, Custis. But you do whatever is necessary. We'll stand behind you."

"All right, Boss. Thanks."

The office door opened and Henry came in without waiting to be invited. He was in shirtsleeves and his hair was wet from melting snow. His cheeks were flushed a bright, blotchy red from the cold outdoors.

"Do you have it?" Vail asked.

"Right here." Henry flashed an envelope.

"A newly signed federal warrant authorizing the arrest of one Cyrus Berman," Billy explained to Longarm. "We don't want to give some lawyer a jurisdictional loophole, so Henry tracked down Judge Franklin and got him to issue the warrant for you to serve. The latest one outstanding was issued almost a year ago in Arkansas, and all we have on it is the process order. I wanted you to have an original in hand just to make sure this Dillmore person or some paid-off local justice of the peace can't balk at the service."

"And I've already worked out your itinerary for travel, Longarm," Henry volunteered. "You take the six-fifteen northbound this evening, connect with the Union Pacific tonight, and catch a late westbound to Bitter Creek, Wyoming. From there you take a feeder stagecoach line. Something called the Wind River Route, whatever that is. It will take you north to Ross County. Don't worry about a ticket. The coach line is a contract mail carrier so they'll honor your badge as a travel pass. As for Talking Water itself"— Henry frowned—" I can't help you there. It isn't on any of the maps I could find here. Still, it has a telegraph line, so it can't be too hard to locate once you get close to it."

"I'll find it."

"I really am sorry about disrupting your weekend," Billy Vail said.

"I didn't mind. Wouldn't have anyway if I'd known it was Berman you had in mind. Besides, far as I know, I'm the only one this side o' Omaha that's ever actually seen the son of a bitch. An' Billy, I wouldn't take a chance on that bastard gettin' away. Not for anything."

"I know, Longarm. Good luck."

Even Henry took the unusual step of reaching out to give Longarm a handshake for luck before handing over the warrant and the expense vouchers Longarm would need.

"Alive or dead, Boss, I'll bring that sonuvabitch in if he's anywhere within a hundred miles o' Talking Water, Wyoming."

10

# Chapter 3

The conductor said it was snowing to beat hell over in the Laramie Mountains, but you couldn't prove it by Longarm. Beyond the oil lamps in the smoking car all he could see was cold emptiness. The U.P. westbound was delayed an hour at Bosler waiting for a snowplow to clear the tracks ahead, but after that it was fast and easy rolling, so open and empty that they were within a quarter hour of the schedule by the time they squealed and rattled to a stop at Bitter Creek in western Wyoming Territory.

Daybreak had come by then, revealing a bleak expanse of grays and browns relieved only occasionally by long windrows of drifted snow. The ground for the most part was bare here, swept clean by the constant winds that also served to evaporate the snow.

This was the South Pass country, the truly high plains where the spine of the great Rocky Mountain chain lay buried beneath a plateau so vast the eye could not detect the altitude. It was called, and indeed appeared to be, a basin. But only because it was ringed on all sides by jagged spires and peaks of mountaintops so tall they carried their snow nearly the full year around.

From horseback, though, or the seat of a passenger coach, this "basin" seemed little different from most rangeland, covered with short grasses and gray sage. Close inspection showed the grasses to be even shorter than normal, however, their stems and foliage smaller and more delicate than the curly buffalo grasses found on the other side of the Bighorns. Longarm had heard a botanist, a man attached to a government survey party, claim that the grass here was some alpine variety with a three-dollar name that the scientist said was Latin, the alpine part meaning that it was supposed to grow only at serious mountain heights. Longarm didn't know about that. Maybe the botanist was right. What Longarm was sure of was that this grass, sparse though it might be, gave plenty of good feeding to whatever livestock or wildlife grazed on it.

Longarm toted his saddle and carpetbag off the rail car and waved away the services of a boy in his teens who offered to carry them for him.

"Tell you what you can do for me t' earn yourself a nickel, son."

"Yes, sir?"

"There's s'posed t' be a stage outfit in town that has a connection north to Ross County."

"Yes, sir, that'd be Sam Jones's Wind River Line."

"I reckon it'd be worth a nickel to me if you'd lead me to Mr. Jones's stage depot."

"You mean that, mister? For certain sure?"

"I said it, son. I meant it."

"You sure you won't back out on me now?"

Longarm cocked his head to one side and gave the kid a close looking over. The boy was grinning. After a few seconds Longarm commenced to grin too. "Don't tell me. We're standing slap beside the place, aren't we?"

"Pret' near," the boy agreed gleefully. "It's the building yonder, right beside the railroad depot here. You woulda seen the sign for yourself if we wasn't standing back here on the platform like this."

Longarm laughed. And reached into his pocket.

"You don't have to do that, mister. I was just having fun with you."

"No harm in that, son. No harm in a man keeping his word neither. I made you a promise and I don't begrudge the nickel." He grinned. "And anyways, the fun was worth that much for the price of admission." He handed the boy his pay, and the kid was bright enough not to refuse it a second time.

Longarm checked in with the stage office and learned the next coach north would leave at noon, weather permitting.

"Twenty hours going north. Some less than that coming back since a lot of the upbound is spend climbing. Easier run coming back, you see. Fare is two dollars and a quarter to Soda Creek, four dollars if you're going to—"

"Whoa. How's about this for my fare." Longarm opened his wallet and displayed his badge.

"I see you got your ticket already, Marshal."

"Just a deputy," Longarm corrected with a smile. "The marshal gets to sit behind a desk in a nice warm office while us deputies go out in the cold till our ears fall off."

"Yes, sir, there's nothing like some nice paperwork and a desk to sit at. You must envy that marshal of yours something fierce."

"Your point is well taken, friend. And I thank you for the reminder."

"You got some time to kill before the coach leaves, Deputy. And you look like too sensible a fellow to have bought any of the pasteboard those butcher boys on the train try to pass off for sandwiches. I know a homey little cafe practically across the street. Warm too, and the best pies and coffee this side of paradise. You can leave your things behind the gate here if you want to go stoke up. I won't let anybody bother them."

"You're mighty kind, friend, and I'll take you up on both offers, the bags and directions to that cafe."

The stage agent smiled. "It's my wife that runs the place, and if it's no trouble, before you leave I'd appreciate you

13

asking her to fetch me over a wedge of her peach pie to go with my coffee.''

Longarm did better than simply tell the lady about her husband's request. When he was done with a truly excellent breakfast he personally carried a plate of pie, still warm from the oven, back to the neighborly man.

# Chapter 4

The coach operated by the Wind River Express and Transit Company—to give it the full title painted in fading yellow over the windows and single side door—was a device of venerable age and experience. It was the standard Concord coach manufactured by Abbot and Downing in Concord, New Hampshire, in a style that had not significantly changed for at least a generation. As this particular vehicle might attest, since it had to be old enough to have carried its current passengers' parents. And maybe their grandparents as well.

Once grand, the old Concord now was worn and sagging. Dry rot showed beneath the varnish along the lower edges of the side panels, and there probably was not a major part on it that had not been replaced time and time again since it first rolled out of the assembly barn. Where once there had been iron hinges on the door, there now were pads of thick leather held haphazardly in place with brass screws so that the door sagged, its latch no longer in proper alignment. To compensate for that, the door was held shut with a twist of wire.

Where once there would have been custom-fitted side curtains with see-through isinglass panels, now there were tattered squares of black canvas tacked over the windows and rolled up, secured with bits of twine until someone decided to let them fall free. Cold as it was, and with dark clouds spreading across the horizon to the west, Longarm suspected they would not get much beyond the town limits of Bitter Creek before the side curtains were let down. Better to put up with the dark than the fierce cold.

The thick, buffalo hide thoroughbraces that served in place of springs no doubt had been replaced many times already as well. And soon would have to be replaced again.

The seats inside—enough to accommodate nine adults in some degree of comfort, or a dozen if they were all feeling real friendly—were worn and shabby. As in virtually all Concords, the middle bench was made to face the rear of the coach, as did the seat built against the driver's box wall. Only the back seat faced forward, and for reasons Longarm never understood this seat was nearly always the one preferred by women passengers. Something to do with their delicate senses not having to ride backward, as it had been explained to him by more than one fair maiden. What he could not comprehend was why it never seemed to occur to any of them that this forward-facing seat was also the one that would fling them onto the laps of any gents riding on the middle bench whenever there was an especially vigorous lurch.

Or then again, he reflected, maybe the ladies did indeed recognize that possibility.

He noticed that the usual row of rooftop seats had been removed from this particular coach and a luggage rack installed instead so freight could be carried in its place. It was a sensible enough change considering the weather. No one who expected to complete a journey alive and unfrozen would want to ride atop a coach exposed to the winter elements, and the income from the extra freight would no doubt help compensate for the loss of outside passenger space.

Longarm had had to ride as a shotgun messenger himself more than once in the past, and could well imagine the

16

sufferings of the jehu and the guard. He did not envy them their constant exposure to the cold, and knew that at this time of year a scheduled ten-minute relay stop would often—and justifiably—become a half hour stop instead while the coach driver and messenger gulped coffee and tried to thaw numb ears and noses.

He gave the Wind River coach a second look, and realized that while the equipment was old and tattered, the things that really counted were well attended. The wheels were solid and properly fitted, with none of the spokes cracked or loose, and the iron tires were all tight-set and in good order. The axles were heavily and freshly greased, and all the running gear appeared to be sound.

As for the items that counted above all others, the mules that would pull the coach seemed sound as well and in excellent health. Their harness was clean and in good repair, and the mules themselves were robust and, unlike a comparable six-up of horses, standing patient in their traces. They were all of good size, in fact rather large for mules, which generally tend to run on the light side. Longarm guessed this team would average nearly nine hundred pounds apiece. And a nine-hundred-pound mule can pull as stoutly as a twelve-hundred-pound horse and do it half again as long. And accomplish this on two thirds the amount of feed.

All in all, Longarm figured himself satisfied with the Wind River Line and its gear as he carried his carpetbag and much-used McClellan saddle out of the stage office and handed them up to the guard, who was helping secure the luggage on the freight rack.

"Careful with the Winchester," Longarm warned when he handed the saddle, rifle scabbard still attached, up to the man. "It's loaded."

"Whyn't you teach your grandma to suck eggs, mister. I was handlin' loaded guns before you was born," the messenger returned in a grumpy tone of voice.

Rather than take offense, Longarm grinned at him.

"Wife have a headache this morning, did she?"

"Got no wife," the messenger said in a slightly more friendly tone. "Got me a helluva hangover, though."

"Think o' the good side of it," Longarm suggested. "The hangover you can get rid of."

The shotgun messenger grinned. He started to laugh out loud, but ended up with a wince instead.

Longarm checked his watch. They had at least twenty minutes before they were supposed to pull out. "You want me to fetch you a cup o' coffee from across the street?"

"You'd do that, mister?"

"Sure. I'd enjoy a cup myself before we leave. Be no trouble to make it two."

"For a cup o' coffee right now, mister, I'd write you inta my will. If I had anything worth leavin', that is."

"Let me get the coffee first. Then I'll make sure you know how t' spell my name right."

The fellow laughed, not even wincing this time, and Longarm ambled back to the cafe for the coffee.

Twenty-five minutes later they were on the road, the messenger and the jehu bundled so deep in scarves and blanket-lined clothing that they looked more like cloth-covered hayricks than human beings. Predictably, the other passengers chose to ride in darkness rather than let in any more breeze than was strictly necessary. Longarm was one of seven passengers making the northbound run, two women and five men. The women were dressed modestly and kept their eyes demurely low, but smears of powder and rouge neglected behind their ears told the truth about their profession. Longarm had no interest in either of them anyway. They were both homely as a pair of mud hens. But then, the further out from polite society the uglier the whores. That seemed to be a law of nature.

Of the men, Longarm guessed one of them to be a salesman of some sort, two who obviously were traveling together he took to be lawyers, and the last was likely a laborer, probably a miner judging by his clothes and destination. Those four plus a United States deputy marshal.

They traveled mostly in silence for the first three-hour relay, and completely in silence for the second. It was miserably cold inside the coach—he could just imagine how bad it must be up top—and the constant jolting and lurching did nothing to relieve that discomfort. By the time they stopped for a late supper at midnight, at a rest station roughly halfway along the route, they were all exhausted and out of sorts. Longarm's bladder was about to bust—at his age he should know better than to drink so much coffee before getting into a stagecoach—and his head was pounding from the effects of the rough ride and unrelenting fatigue.

Still, a good piss, a better cigar, and a steaming bowl of beef stew can do wonders to restore body and spirit alike. By the time they rolled out again he felt damn near human.

And damn near dead all over again by the time they reached McCarthy Falls, the seat of Ross County. That was at four-thirty in the morning, 4:22 to be precise about it, and a light snow had begun to fall. Light as to the number of flakes, that is. But the snowflakes themselves were unusually large, soft, and wet.

Except for one or two falls very early in the snow season, and one or two more very late, snow in the high country is normally very dry, the flakes exceptionally small and without substance. Powder, it is generally called, and powder is what it most resembles. Pick up a shovel full of high country snow and all you feel is the weight of the shovel.

This snow, however, was unusually moist and weighty. If a snow like this intensified or simply continued to fall for a long time, Longarm knew, it could create problems.

"Naw, don't worry y'self none," the jehu assured him when Longarm mentioned the weather. "We'll be safe in Talking Water before anything short of a regular blizzard could bother us."

Longarm accepted the driver's judgment, local knowledge being more valuable than any amount of generality,

19

and remained seated while the two whores and one of the lawyers got off in McCarthy Falls.

Normal practice really should have had Longarm leaving the stagecoach there too.

Custom calls for a federal peace officer to give local lawmen the courtesy of a howdy before attending to business within another man's jurisdiction.

In this case, however, with Sheriff Dillmore balking at the arrest of Cy Berman, Longarm decided the best course of action would be for him to go straight on to Talking Water and take Berman into custody first. Then, but only then, he might consider dropping by to have a word with Dillmore.

A man wearing a bearskin coat—and smelling about as ripe as a bear fresh out of hibernation too—got in to take up the space that previously had been occupied by the whores. All in all, Longarm would have preferred the company of the whores. At least they hadn't stunk. Still, it should only be a few more hours to Talking Water. Then he could look up this tipster who wrote to Billy, and finally put Cyrus Berman where the cocksucker most properly belonged. Either behind bars or underground. Far as Custis Long was concerned, one would be every bit as good as the other.

The wind-stiff driver and guard, both of them looking like they'd been sprinkled with salt now that the wet snowflakes were beginning to adhere to them, climbed back on top with groans of protest, and soon the coach rocked and jolted into motion once more, taking the road onto the south slopes of Mount Harwood.

Somewhere on the other side of a pass called Goshen there was supposed to be the gold camp of Talking Water.

And whatever Longarm would find there.

# Chapter 5

It was snowing like a sonuvabitch by the time they reached Talking Water. The big, wet flakes were floating down with virtually no wind to disturb their fall, and at least a foot and a half of the soft, mushy, barely frozen snow had accumulated. Someone had gone to the trouble to build snow-sheds in those places where drifts were likely to develop, but with no wind the sheds were not really needed now.

The mules plodded doggedly through, their pace hampered but by no means halted, and Talking Water was reached shortly after eleven a.m., stretching the trip from its normal twenty hours to something approaching twenty-four.

The jehu and his guard looked like walking, talking snowmen by the time they climbed down off the box. Yet oddly, they moved and acted more comfortably now than they had before the storm struck. It took Longarm a few moments to figure out why. Despite the miserable-looking conditions, the temperature was actually higher now, and therefore easier to take, than when they'd pulled out of Bitter Creek the day before.

As for Talking Water, it was about what one would expect of a rough and ready mining camp. The buildings were mostly dugouts or aspen log cabins, which in itself was

21

enough to proclaim the residents' expectations for the future. Any man who builds with aspen expects a short stay because aspen wood is soft and deteriorates quickly. A man who expects to stay a while will go to the trouble to work with pine and ignore the more plentiful and easily cut aspen.

Even in February, Longarm noticed, there were some businesses with aspen walls and canvas tenting roofs here. It seemed no one expected Talking Water to last more than another few summers. At most.

When the gold disappeared so would all the people, and a few years after that it would be difficult to find any structure standing more than waist high, except possibly for the remnants of a chimney here and there. And even most of those were stick-and-mud affairs that would fall apart soon enough and disappear right along with the cabins they now warmed.

This, Longarm knew, was what passed for progress in the gold country.

As for the name of the town, that became obvious as soon as he stood on the long, narrow street that ran through the camp. Talking Water was situated along the banks of a very fast-moving creek that leaped and burbled its way through a steeply falling valley, a defile deep enough and narrow enough that in many places it would be called a gulch or cut or gully. Or in some places back East, a holler.

Whatever one wanted to term the declivity through which the stream passed, the swift-moving water bounced and bubbled its way over rocks and boulders, and the sounds of its passage left no doubt as to the source of the community's name. The bright waters did indeed seem to "talk." And in a most musical and pleasant voice at that. The sounds of the stream lay like a constant undertone all through the little valley.

Longarm suspected Talking Water had been pretty when the gold here was first discovered. Now, of course, it was drab and ugly, and would have been even worse to the eye had it not been for the clean, white blanket of snow that hid most of the frozen mud from view.

Since the coming of the mines and the miners, every stick of wood within sight had been cut down and used, whether for construction or tunnel shoring or simply for firewood. Now only dirt and stone and the leavings of careless humankind would be visible once the snow melted. It was a damned shame in a way, Longarm thought, but necessary. The price of progress.

But a damned shame nonetheless.

Longarm accepted his things from the now-friendly shotgun guard, who had long since recovered from his hangover.

"Any suggestions on where a fellow could take a room?" Longarm asked.

"That one is easy to answer, mister. Only one place in town as rents rooms. There's a boardinghouse upcreek a quarter mile or so. Four bits including two meals. But you got to share your bed, an' everybody sleeps in the one big room sorta like a barracks."

Longarm made a face. Apart from personally despising any such arrangement, he knew it would present a problem if—when—he had a prisoner to oversee through the night. Some measure of privacy was needed, or at least of control, if he was going to keep Cyrus Berman's pals, if any, from posing a threat.

"There's one other possibility," the messenger added when he saw Longarm's disappointment.

"Yes, friend?"

"Me and Jesse have cots in the tack room inside the stage line barn over there. If you can make do with a pallet laid on the floor, you're welcome to stay with us. No charge."

"That's mighty nice o' you."

"Don't think nothing of it."

"Well, I do. And I thank you."

The shotgun guard seemed shyly pleased that his invitation had been accepted. Longarm suspected the man would be even more pleased with the gift of a bottle this evening by way of a real thank-you. Longarm reminded himself to bring one along with him when he came to bed later.

"I'm going that way anyhow. Be glad to take your things with me," the guard offered.

"Then that's another thing I've to thank you for."

The guard jumped down to the ground and took Longarm's bag and saddle. "We won't bolt the door, so come in any time you've a mind to."

"Thanks." Longarm touched the brim of his flat-crowned Stetson and turned away. When he did so he opened the second and third buttons from the bottom on his coat. Not that he was expecting any trouble at the moment. But a man never knows when he might want to get at his belly gun in a hurry. Hell, if there was warning ahead of time, the gun wouldn't likely be necessary in the first place.

He found a cafe and stopped in to warm himself with coffee and a huge breakfast, and while he was waiting for the meal to be served, dug through his pockets for the envelope Billy Vail had given him back in Denver.

The man who'd written to say Cy Berman was here, and that he could point Berman out, had signed his letter "A. Brownlee." The return address was "General Delivery, Talking Water, W.T."

Soon he was done eating, Longarm figured, he would look up this A. Brownlee person.

And then Cyrus Berman first thing after.

# Chapter 6

Longarm laid a quarter on the table to cover the cost of his meal, then stood, pausing for another moment to take one last, satisfying swallow of hot coffee before bundling up in readiness for the cold outside.

He heard the front door open, and when he turned in that direction saw the slim form of a very shapely young woman who was engaged in fussily arranging her cloak on the coat rack beside the entry. She had dark auburn hair drawn back in a tight bun. A little closer to the floor she had a different sort of tight bun, small and rounded and mighty shapely. Longarm took a moment to enjoy the view, then put his hat on and strode forward.

The woman turned just as he passed her. Longarm's attention was directed very carefully toward the door lest he give offense.

But he could not help catching the movement out of the corner of his eye when with a gasp the lady's hand flew to her throat as if in alarm.

He stopped. Looked. And his eyes widened as the look turned into a stare.

"Custis!"

"Madelyn? Maddy? Is it really . . . ?"

"Is it really . . . ?" she echoed almost in unison with his words.

Both stared a moment longer. And then Maddy Williams shook her head. "No. Please, no." Blindly she whirled and grabbed her cloak off the rack. She did not even take time to swing it over her shoulders before she bolted out into the swirling snowstorm.

Longarm did not want to make her afraid that he was following, so he took his time about trimming and lighting a cheroot. Only then did he step out into the bitter cold and go on his way.

"You took your by-God time about showing up here. The stage came in near two hours ago."

"Yes, and now it's gone again. In case you're interested, Berman wasn't on it. I watched t' make sure," Longarm answered.

"How the hell would you know that? I'm the one can point him out."

"I'd know," Longarm said. He felt no compulsion to give this sloppy, slovenly, sorry excuse for a human any explanations. But he would indeed know Cy Berman if or when he saw the man.

Longarm had known Berman years ago. They'd once, if briefly, worked together punching cows on an outfit in the sand hills of Nebraska. That was before Berman became a murderer and before Custis Long came to be known as Longarm. Back then Cy Berman had only been a petty thief and a would-be gunman. Custis had caught him at the thieving part of his profession, pilfering another hand's bedroll, and had called him on it. Berman had thought about trying Long. That much had been plain in the ugly look in Berman's eyes. But the man hadn't had the nerve to stand belly to belly and eye to eye. Shoot or crawl, those had been the choices. Berman had crawled. Rolled his bed and sloped out of there without so much as finding the foreman to draw his final pay. Longarm hadn't seen the bastard since.

26

But he would know Berman when he did see him. There was no question about that.

All of that was personal, though, and nothing he would care to explain for the satisfaction of a man like Adrian Brownlee.

"You sure he wasn't on that stage?"

"I said it once. Don't ask me again."

"No call for you to be tetchy."

Longarm had gone from the cafe back to the stage office, where a new crew and fresh mules were due to take the coach on the turnaround. The stage line operated two coaches on the Bitter Creek to Talking Water run, giving them a daily schedule in each direction. The same driver and guard who had brought Longarm north today would sleep over in Talking Water tonight and take the southbound route tomorrow, driving past the coach that should be preparing to pull out of Bitter Creek at just about the same time this one was leaving Talking Water. The two would pass sometime during the night, but likely the drivers and guards would be the only ones awake enough to realize it. Longarm hadn't ever seen the southbound when they'd passed it some hours earlier.

He'd been pleased to learn there was such frequent service, though, because it meant he would not have to be stuck here waiting to take Berman out.

Even after learning about the schedule, however, he had been concerned that the storm might delay travel. The friendly guard, George Magler, had assured him there would be no problem. "There's only a few places subject to serious drift, an' we got the snowsheds finished in those spots. You seen 'em when we was coming in, didn't you?"

"I seen 'em," Longarm had acknowledged.

"I never yet seen snow on the flat so deep these mules can't pull through it. And I got a shovel to use if we run into a windrow or something like that. But we'll get through, all right. We never been late with a mail delivery yet, summer nor winter neither one."

"That's an impressive record."

"One we ain't gonna lose neither. Trust us. We'll make 'er through on time."

So Longarm had waited and watched while the south-bound passengers boarded, then looked up the postmaster for directions to Adrian Brownlee's shallow-scratch gold mine. If one wanted to dignify such a tiny hole in the ground by that name. After getting a good look at Brownlee, Longarm suspected the man was more interested in drinking up the little gold he found than in wasting time and energy searching for more of the yellow metal. Longarm suspected that a pair of twelve-year-old boys with hand trowels and an oak bucket could dig a better hole over one summer's weekend than Brownlee had dug here in however much time he'd had his claim.

Still, Longarm hadn't come here to criticize A. Brownlee but to enlist the man's assistance. And that was a thing he had best keep in mind.

He rearranged his expression to something more friendly and said, "I hope you know how much we appreciate your, uh, public spirit and cooperation."

"It ain't your thanks that I want, Deputy. It's the seven hundred dollars in rewards that's posted for Berman. That's right, ain't it? Seven hundred?"

"Actually I think it's eight hundred fifty, but I suppose I could be wrong about that."

Brownlee smiled for the first time since he'd climbed out of his prospect hole.

"That's what drew your interest in this?" Longarm asked. "The rewards?"

"Sure, what else? I don't give a shit about Berman in particular. It's nothing personal with me, see. What I do, I go to post offices now an' then an' study them wanted flyers. Pays off too. I made fifty dollars once back in Kentucky an' three hundred off a fella over in Idaho. This Berman, he'll be my best catch ever."

"I see."

28

"Nothing wrong with it, is there?"

"No, of course not. Like I told you, Mr. Brownlee, me and the marshal, we appreciate all the help we can get from, uh, citizens."

"Just see you appreciate it eight hundred fifty dollars worth."

"Quick as Berman is in custody I'll wire for your authorizations. After that I'm not responsible. But I'll do right by you."

Brownlee scowled. "You ain't said nothing about your split of the rewards."

"No split. Federal officers aren't allowed."

"I've heard that. I've also knowed fellows that've had to pay shares to deputy marshals."

"Not working out of the Denver district, I bet."

"I wouldn't know about that shit."

"I would."

"So anyhow, you wanta go see your boy Berman?"

"That's what I came all this way to do, Mr. Brownlee. It surely is."

"Lemme change outa these gum rubber boots an' I'll take you to the son of a bitch. It won't take me but a minute."

# Chapter 7

A pale woman at the general mercantile said her man could be found at home this afternoon. She gave Brownlee a look of undisguised fear when she said it. But then, Longarm remembered, it was no secret here that Brownlee was accusing the man who called himself Thomas Gedrey of being Cy Berman.

"I know where he lives," Brownlee said. "C'mon."

Longarm made the mistake of looking into the woman's haunted, stricken face. Then he followed Brownlee out, realizing too late that he should have thought to enter the store by himself.

Brownlee pointed. "It's right around the corner here. We'll go to the side door. That's where a neighbor would call."

Longarm nodded. He didn't much like Adrian Brownlee. But the man's advice on that point was sound. A knock at the front door is always more suspicious than one at the kitchen.

As they walked around the side of the small house Longarm reached inside his coat and withdrew the Colt, holding the blued-steel revolver low at his side where it would be ready without being obvious.

He motioned for Brownlee to stand away, then approached the door and tapped lightly on it.

Inside the house he could hear the scrape of chair legs on a bare floor and the approach of footsteps.

The man who very slowly and cautiously pulled the door open was of middle age, with graying hair and a pencil-thin mustache. He was in shirtsleeves, wearing a flannel shirt with the cuffs rolled back off strong forearms.

There was a star-shaped badge pinned over the left breast pocket of his shirt.

The man held a stubby shotgun that had been cut down to pistol size. A 16-gauge, Longarm guessed. And one lethal little sonuvabitch at close range.

"I take it you'd be Sheriff Dillmore," Longarm observed.

"I would. And you?"

"Deputy United States marshal out o' the Denver district. The name is Long. I'll be glad t' show my badge if you like. I can reach for it slow an' easy."

"Long, you say?"

"That's right."

"You got a nickname?"

"Longarm."

"I've heard of you. They say you're straight-arrow."

"I'd like to think whoever says that is right," Longarm replied.

"They say you'll give a man a chance before you shoot."

Longarm nodded. "Any that'll let me. I get no pleasure from another man's hurt."

"Tom. Step over here and show yourself. Long, I'd appreciate it if you'd take a good look at this man before you do anything that can't be undone."

As a show of good faith the sheriff of Ross County laid his ugly little shotgun on a nearby lamp stand and stepped back two paces.

From the far side of the Gedrey kitchen a man stepped out of the shadows.

Longarm's belly muscles contracted.

And then turned loose.

"By God," he declared. "You sure as hell look like enough to the man t' be his brother. Damn near like enough to be his twin."

"You know Berman?" Dillmore asked.

"I do."

"Well enough to know this ain't him?"

"Ayuh, I know him that well. And I never seen this fellow before."

Both Dillmore and Gedrey visibly relaxed. "Come in out of the cold, Marshal, and join us for some coffee."

No such invitation was extended to Adrian Brownlee, but he came in out of the snow too.

"Why did you come all this way, Longarm, when I wired your boss there was no need?"

"Your wire didn't say much."

"Said all that needed saying. There wasn't cause to arrest Tom here. That's what I told him. At twenty-six cents a word too. You got any idea what my budget is? Believe me, you don't want to know. I sent him what was necessary in the wire, and followed that with a letter explaining everything. Three cents to mail the whole letter. Twenty-six cents a damn word for the wire. With my budget the marshal is lucky he got any wire at all."

Longarm decided the best idea here would be to let Dillmore get his story out in his own good time. Besides, the coffee was good.

"This man is Thomas Andrew Gedrey. He's named for his grampa Thomas Dillmore and his uncle Andrew Dillmore. I'm A.T. to my friends. To you too if you like. I'm named for my father Andrew and my grampa Thomas. My father and Tom's mother are brother and sister. So I've known Tom all his life and mine. I told Mr. Brownlee here that Tom isn't his man Berman. He didn't believe me. I—"

"But the son of a bitch looks so much like Berman!"

Brownlee didn't have time to say more. Gedrey was out of his chair in a flash and had Brownlee by the scruff of the neck, hauling him away from the table like you would an unruly dog.

Adrian Brownlee was half a foot taller than Tom Gedrey and probably forty pounds heavier. Gedrey threw him bodily out the side door and into the snow as easily as if he'd been discarding a pail of used dishwater.

"Sorry about that," he said when he returned to the table.

"No need t' apologize," Longarm said. "It's your table. I don't see as you need to accept insults at it."

Gedrey grunted and sat hunched over his coffee.

"You really do look an awful lot like Berman," Longarm observed. "But he has a meanness in him that pinches his mouth and puts cruelty in his eyes. There's none o' that in you. I'm sorry you had t' be bothered. But with a man like Berman we'd do anything it takes t' bring him in. I hope you know there's no ill will toward you. Just toward that murderer Berman."

"I understand that. No hard feelings." Gedrey reached forward to shake on that.

"No hard feelings," Longarm affirmed.

But dammit, he surely did wish it had been Cyrus Berman in this gold camp after all.

Dammit.

Gedrey brightened and sat up straighter in his chair. "Tell you what, Deputy. Why don't I cut us each a piece of my Edna's pie to go with this coffee. She bakes a might fine pie if I do say it on her."

"It'd be my pleasure, Mr. Gedrey."

"Tom," the recent suspect corrected as he went to get the pie.

"Fine, Tom. An' it's Longarm to you an' A.T. here."

# Chapter 8

Failure was not exactly what Longarm had hoped to report to Billy Vail, but failure—at least in a manner of speaking—was his result here. Cyrus Berman was still out there somewhere, free to rob and murder and thumb his nose at all the deputies who wanted so badly to nail his ears over their mantle.

Longarm got directions from A.T. Dillmore, and found the telegraph office housed in a cubicle at the back end of the small shop that also included what passed for the post office in Talking Water. Apart from being a part-time telegrapher and postal clerk, the proprietor of the shop made shoes, repaired harness, sharpened knives or scissors, and for all Longarm knew read palms and told fortunes too. But he was just guessing about those last two. All the rest was documented by the myriad signs posted inside the shop and out. It was probably because there were so many signs and any one of them could get lost amid all the confusion that he hadn't noticed the telegraph office sign when he'd been there earlier seeking directions to Adrian Brownlee's place from the post office.

The man nodded when Longarm stepped inside and stamped the wet, clinging snow off his boots.

"Ach now, you could've told me before that you're the

34

deputy marshal sent up from Denver, couldn't ye?''

''If I'd thought it was important. But how'd you find out about it in the last hour or so?''

The shoemaker/tinker grinned. ''There aren't a lot of secrets in a town this size, Marshal. Word traveled just about as quick as the stagecoach did, starting right from the time when you showed a badge instead of buying a ticket down in Bitter Creek.''

''How the hell . . . ?''

''That's the sort of thing gets talked about, you know. Gossip spreads faster than fire. That's gospel.'' The shopkeeper chuckled. ''The only surprise is that I hadn't got the word on you before you came in earlier. And you in town long enough to have a meal at Fred's cafe too.''

Longarm shook his head and smiled. There wasn't much else he could do actually. And anyway, it wasn't like there was any reason to try and keep his job a secret. Everyone who might have cause to care already knew anyway.

''Since I see I'm right about you being the marshal, can I tell you what you came in here to do?''

Shit, maybe he'd been right about this fortune-teller stuff after all. ''Sure, go ahead.''

''Those boots look to be in fine shape, so you didn't come in for a repair job. And I doubt you have scissors to sharpen. Since Tom Gedrey isn't the man Ad Brownlee claimed—and before you ask, most of the town knew all about that before you ever thought about coming up here— well, since all that's the case, you won't be staying in this godforsaken little hole in the mountains long enough to send or receive mail. So what I conclude, Marshal, is that you've come to send a telegram. To take it one step more, my guess is that you'll be wanting to report back to your boss that Tom wasn't your man. That's so they know to keep on looking someplace else for the fellow.'' The man's smile was positively beatific as he basked in the pleasures of deduction. And of perhaps a smidgen of showing off too.

"I'd say you're doing right fine, friend," Longarm allowed. "I'm impressed." Which was obviously the sort of thing the fellow wanted to hear.

"Always glad to please," the tinker/telegrapher said. "But I'm afraid that is the only satisfaction you'll get here today."

"Pardon?"

"Oh, it isn't my desire to disappoint. Certainly not. But I'm afraid the telegraph line is down somewhere between here and Soda Spring. I can't even raise McCarthy Falls."

Longarm frowned.

"Sorry, Marshal, but it's a common enough problem. The contractor who put in the wire was one of those who cut every corner and shaved flakes of copper off every penny before he'd spend it. He used too fine a wire in the telegraph line, so the tensile strength is not what it should be. That makes the line vulnerable to breakage. What's worse, every place he could he left the road and strung wire across shortcuts. Through canyons and over ridges and such. He saved the price of some poles and likely a few miles of wire. But he also made it hard for repair crews to follow the line and look for breaks at this time of year. And on top of that, he took the wire through some thick timber, what we call up here black timber, that dense stuff where the big elk hang out. In conditions like this when the snow is wet and heavy, the limbs overload and can break and come down on the wire. And being weak and brittle to begin with, the wire snaps all too easy. We get breaks enough even after a regular snow. In conditions like this I wouldn't be surprised if there was ten or fifteen different places that will have to be located and spliced before we have telegraph service restored. Could be out a week or even longer, there's no way to tell."

"Your knowledge impresses me, friend, but your news disappoints."

"Sorry, Marshal. I would change it if I could." He smiled again. "Or if it makes you feel better, I could lie to you. I'm fairly good at that when I want to be."

Longarm laughed. "Nice o' you t' offer but I reckon I'll pass. Tell you what you could do, though. You could tell me where a man might find a good grade o' Maryland rye whiskey in this town." It occurred to Longarm that a man who talked as freely as did this shoemaker must be lonely, so he added, "Better yet, if you have the time you could show me. I'd enjoy the company if you'd join me for a dram or three."

The sometime telegrapher beamed with a flush of sudden pleasure. "Give me two seconds to close the shop, Marshal, and I'll show you the best our budding burg has to offer."

"Sounds good t' me, friend."

# Chapter 9

Longarm was . . . mellow. Not drunk. Far from that. But for
sure the rough edges had been smoothed out a mite.

It had been a nice afternoon and evening. Tom and A.T.
had come by the table. And half-a-dozen other gents after
them. Longarm had lost maybe seventy-five cents in an
amiable game of stud poker, and won back thirty of it later
playing draw, all of it penny-ante, just a friendly way to
pass the time.

The whiskey had been good. Not the Maryland distilled
product that he favored, but near enough to it in quality.
The liquor available here came from Pennsylvania—some
town outside Philadelphia, one of the other boys had said—
and it was smooth on the tongue and warm in the belly.
Definitely better than the bat piss they bottled in New Jer-
sey and sold to an unsuspecting public.

And wonder of wonders, the saloon kept a stock of cigars
so pale and plump they shouldn't be smoked but mounted
on walls like the works of art they properly were. Longarm
was smoking one of them as he walked slowly to the mule
barn where he would be sleeping tonight.

He was in no hurry. The snow had stopped and although
it was cold, there was no real bite to the air. The humidity
was high so the cold was more soft than stinging. He hadn't

even bothered to button his coat or turn the collar high.

George, the friendly shotgun guard, and his jehu partner, Jesse, were both back at the watering hole Longarm had just left. They'd told him to turn in whenever he wanted, that they would be along later.

At the moment Longarm was pleasantly tired. He hadn't gotten any sleep to speak of the night before while riding in the jolting stagecoach, and unlike George and the driver, had not spent the afternoon sleeping. He figured to crawl into the sack early tonight and get a good sleep because tomorrow night he would be on the southbound coach run and would get no rest then.

He reached the barn and stopped outside, leaning against the front wall instead of going directly in to find his bed. There are some things a thoughtful man does not do. And walking into another man's barn with a lighted cigar or pipe is one of them.

And this smoke was much too good to discard half finished.

Besides, the evening was a pleasant one, the heavy storm clouds gone now and the stars starkly bright against the black velvet of the night sky above.

Longarm stuffed his hands into his pockets and leaned contentedly back against the split aspen wall, crossing his boots at the ankles and enjoying the feel of a gentle breeze against the side of his neck. The moving air was cool but not chilling, almost comforting in the lightness of its touch.

He drew deep on his cigar, held the smoke in his lungs for a moment, and then opened his mouth wide to puff out a string of white, wispy smoke rings. The circles of smoke hung in the air for only moments before they were picked up by the breeze and floated away, their shape elongating and twisting. Longarm watched one ring turn and distort until it took on the appearance of a figure eight. He opened his mouth to blow some more.

And froze in place.

39

A chill swept through him that had nothing to do with the mild air temperature.

Behind him, barely inches away on the other side of the barn wall, he'd heard movement.

And it wasn't a mule that had made the noise either.

This had been human. Guaranteed.

A cough? Not really. Nor a suppressed cough. More like a faint, muffled choking sound.

Choking. Someone trying to hold back the sound. Someone not inside the tack room where Longarm and the stagecoach crew would be sleeping, but inside the barn itself.

Somebody waiting in there who didn't want to make any noise that would announce his presence.

Longarm's senses were instantly alert, his easygoing lassitude discarded so completely it might never have existed.

He tried to remember. He'd glanced inside the barn earlier in the afternoon, but only briefly. He hadn't given any particular thought to it, merely wanting to know where it was he would be bedding down for the night.

Now he wished he'd paid more attention.

He let the partially smoked cigar drop unheeded into the soft snow at his feet, and gave a moment of thankful thought to the presence of the snow. Being so soft and deep, it acted like a thick layer of sawdust that would have to completely muffle the sounds of footsteps.

He had to assume that whoever was inside the barn knew he—or someone—was outside. Hell, he'd been obvious enough about it, announcing his presence with the smoke from his cigar that would be all too easily smelled by anyone who was even halfway alert.

And an ambusher damn sure has his senses tuned to as high a pitch as he can reach.

The guy should know that Longarm was there, then. But with luck he wouldn't be able to hear when Longarm slipped away.

Slowly, careful to make no sound in the soft, deadening snow, he eased away from the wall and moved to his left, turning to round the corner of the barn and head toward the back.

He slipped between the bars of the corral and approached the back door, left open so the mules could come inside to shelter or go out again as they pleased.

The snow inside the corral had been churned into a brown mush by the feet of the mules, and the ground was not completely hard beneath this slop. Longarm could still move in it quietly, but had to be careful lest he lose his footing on the slippery surface and take a tumble. That would be sure to warn the ambusher. And he damn sure did not want that.

He ducked under the neck of one mule and eased past the flank of another, then palmed his Colt and, bracing himself in case the ambusher happened to be looking down the center alleyway, stepped inside.

There was no gunfire. No sound of alarm. Nothing but the dull, plopping footfalls of a mule leaving the hayrack and passing Longarm on its way outdoors.

The presence of the mules was a blessing, he knew. Their movement would mask his and their sounds would already have made the ambusher insensitive to the happenings at the back end of the barn. That was all to the good.

What was not so good was that the ambusher's vision would be thoroughly adjusted by now to the dark interior of the barn, while Longarm was still accustomed to the relatively bright outdoors with its starlight and the flare of lamps inside nearby windows reflecting brightly off the newfallen snow.

Still, he was inside now and undetected.

He paused for a moment, waiting until another mule began to move about, then ghosted forward through the alley past closed stall doors.

A heavy gate blocked the front of the alley, containing the mules in the back two thirds of the barn area while the front third held the tack room and large work area where animals could be harnessed, doctored, groomed, whatever they required.

The ambusher was somewhere in that front third of the building, probably still close beside the wall to the left of the big double doors. At least that was where he'd been when Longarm had heard him swallow back that impulse to cough.

Longarm crouched in the straw that had been cast over the barn floor and, revolver at the ready, closed his eyes in an effort to speed the adjustment of his night vision.

Somewhere ahead he heard another faint choking sound, and then another. A man oughtn't to set himself up in ambush if he's got a cold, Longarm thought. Not, that is, that he wanted this particular ambusher to get any better at his stealthy trade. Longarm was glad enough to take advantage of whatever mistakes the bastard wanted to make.

He heard a slight shuffling of feet on hard earth. Then the ambusher moved and Longarm could at least see where he was.

He'd come back against the wall of the forward-most stall, the one across the alley to Longarm's right.

Getting in position to open up with a shotgun as soon as Longarm opened the doors to come in to bed? That's the way Longarm would have planned it if their situations had been reversed.

Get back away from the door and to the side away from the tack room so the victim's attention would be aimed in that other direction.

Then open up as soon as those doors swung apart.

A load of single-aught buckshot in the belly will damn near chop a man in two. Do it like that and you never have to worry about return fire, for there sure as hell won't be any.

But that was only if the guy got his shot off.

Longarm knew he couldn't trust opening the alley gate, nor the stall door either. He would have liked to get behind

42

the ambusher at close range so he could take him by surprise. And take him alive.

The thing was, Longarm had no enemies here that he knew about. And if someone was gunning for him he'd like to find out the who and the why of it. That would best be done if he could take the guy alive.

He'd do that if he could.

What he needed now was patience. Take his time and stay right where he was. Let the guy get bored and come to him. All the ambusher had to do was move ten, twelve feet to his left and Longarm could reach across the gate and snake an arm around the guy's throat from behind. Nice, silent, and safe. No problem at all.

The ambusher choked again.

Choke, Longarm found himself thinking. He couldn't himself tell why he insisted on thinking of it as the ambusher choking. Not coughing but choking. Yet not quite that either. That was puzzling. But not so much so that he was going to waste any time worrying about it.

All he had to do now was be patient.

Eventually the guy was bound to wonder what had become of the person who'd stood outside smoking a cigar a little while ago.

Or even if the guy was so insensitive to what was around him that he'd somehow missed smelling that smoke, surely he would become restless sooner or later and move the few feet Longarm needed in order to reach him and wrap him up without anybody dying.

Surely he . . .

Longarm felt a cold emptiness in his belly. He could hear voices outside. Coming this way. George and Jesse. He recognized the sounds of their voices. They were coming in to go to bed.

In another few seconds one of them would grab hold of the barn doors and pull them open.

And one, maybe both of those men would likely die.

Even if Longarm was the target, the ambusher would be too keyed up to hold back.

As soon as those doors opened, dammit, somebody was likely to die.

Longarm had no choice. Not if he wanted to keep two innocent men from being cut down.

Without pausing to think about the danger to himself, he bounded to his feet and, taking two long strides to build speed as he crossed the alleyway, launched himself over the gate at the dark, shadowy figure of the ambusher.

# Chapter 10

Noise. There was no way to cover that much distance in a rush without making noise. No way to do it without warning the sonuvabitch what was happening.

And it takes but an instant to turn and yank a trigger. Longarm's only chance was to startle the bastard so much that it would immobilize him.

A moment was all that he needed.

But that moment of stunned hesitation he absolutely had to have.

As he threw himself over the gate he let out a roar. A deep, bone-chilling howl that started in his belly and ripped out of his throat.

He wanted—needed—the shock and the surprise of the attack to freeze the ambusher. Otherwise . . .

He saw the dim form turn and raise one arm as if to ward off Longarm's charge.

Or perhaps to raise a weapon.

Longarm could not see and did not have time to worry about it anyway.

He hit the ambusher chest high, all of Longarm's weight bearing down, and both of them were propelled in a tangle of arms and legs, grunts and grimaces, onto a pile of sour straw.

No sooner had Longarm's paralyzing shout died away than it was replaced by a high-pitched shriek of raw terror coming from somewhere close to Longarm's right ear.

He didn't have time to think about that. He had the gunman to deal with.

Quickly, before the ambusher could have time to recover, Longarm tried to throw a punch. The two were much too close together. There was neither space nor leverage for such a blow, and his punch landed ineffectually on the muscle pad of the ambusher's shoulder.

Longarm tried again, this time with a viciously chopping elbow that caught the ambusher on the left temple. Longarm felt his opponent's head snap back and the body beneath his suddenly go limp as the ambusher was knocked unconscious.

Before he had time to rise or even to turn, he was jumped from behind.

Longarm twisted and kicked out at his attacker.

He heard a yelp of pain. And a familiar voice. He stopped fighting and let the hard hands of George and the stage driver pull him away from the limp body of the would-be ambusher.

"Longarm?" A match flared and he could see the two men he had leaped into action to save. The door to the barn stood open, cold air sweeping inside unheeded.

The stage driver gave Longarm a look of undisguised disgust. "I never woulda took you for a rapist, damn you."

"Pardon me?" Longarm had no idea what the idiot could mean by a remark like that.

The driver pointed toward the form lying motionless at their feet. The gesture extinguished the match he had been holding in the same hand, and it took several moments before George could locate a lantern and light it.

"Oh, shit," Longarm said.

It was no ambusher with a shotgun that was lying there but Madelyn Williams.

"I thought . . ." he began. His subsequent explanation

46

sounded lame even in his own ears, and he did not blame the driver for seeming skeptical after its telling. George was more charitable, but even he needed some convincing.

It was Maddy herself who confirmed Longarm's story when she finally came around. She had a knot above her left ear, but the skin was not broken and she seemed little worse for the experience.

"It's true I was standing here in the dark. Hiding, you might say. I didn't want anyone to know I was coming around here at night to talk with a man in private. You can understand that, surely. People would talk. You know how they can be. I came inside here where I thought it would be warmer and waited in the dark so no one would know. I never thought about Custis mistaking me for someone who could want to do him harm. I was just standing there. And then the next thing I knew there was this awful roaring shout and someone or something leaping at me. That's when I screamed."

"We heard that an' come runnin', miss. Didn't take no special thought to hear 'twas a woman afraid that was doin' the screamin'," Jesse said.

"We thought Longarm was ... you know," George added lamely.

"You were very brave, rushing in to save me like that. Thank you."

Both men looked pleased, and Longarm thought George might be blushing a little at the pretty girl's thanks.

"Could I ask you something, Miz Bell?"

"Yes, certainly."

Longarm was mildly puzzled. Miss Bell, the driver had called her. Maddy's name was Williams. Or had been when Longarm knew her down in Telluride. There could be any number of reasons why she might choose to call herself something different here, of course.

"You called this man here by his first name a moment back. I'm thinking maybe you two already know each other?"

It was Maddy's turn to blush. And there was no question about it. She turned a bright scarlet as the heat of embarrassment rushed into her rounded cheeks.

"Might be, miss, that you shouldn't let that be known around town. You know what I'm saying? Folks here wouldn't think anything special 'bout a lady in your, um, particular circumstances needin' to have you a word with a deputy Ewe Ess marshal. But if they thought you was talking 'bout something personal, well, that'd be different the way they might be looking at it. You know? Me and George here, we won't say nothing to nobody. You have my word on that. How 'bout you, George?"

"Mine too," the shotgun guard pledged.

"But you might oughta keep that in mind, miss."

"That's twice tonight you've been nice enough to try and save me," Maddy said, and touched the driver on the wrist. The man looked acutely uncomfortable with that small amount of intimacy. And immeasurably pleased.

"George and me are gonna go back to the saloon and play another couple hands of poker now. Reckon the two o' you can use the room over there to do your talking. It's warm an' private an' there's places to set. Longarm, whyn't you drop over to the saloon later an' have a drink with us before we all turn in." Which was Jesse's polite way of saying he and George would stay the hell away as long as was necessary. And no questions about what might, or might not, be happening in the tack room in the meantime.

"You're mighty thoughtful," Longarm said. "Thanks."

"No trouble."

George handed Longarm the lantern, and Jesse led the way out of the barn, carefully shutting the door behind them and leaving Longarm alone with Madelyn . . . or whatever it was she was calling herself these days.

Maddy followed Longarm into the tack room, where two cots and a pallet were made up.

She looked at the larger of the cots.

And blushed again as she turned to face Longarm and lifted her eyes to meet his.

48

# Chapter 11

Longarm had no idea what was going through Maddy's mind at that moment, but his own mind was very clear.

He was remembering.

Seeing her eyes. But close to his. Only inches from his own. Cornflower blue, huge and bright and trusting.

And that trim, tidy, tiny body of hers. Naked. Her skin cool to the touch. Her breasts pink-tipped, the size of wild plums in August, barely a mouthful. But firm. And tasty.

Her belly flat and soft above a mat of dark curls.

The lips of her pussy an even brighter pink than that of her nipples. And wet. Slick and shiny with the moisture of quick desire.

Her laughter—Maddy Williams was always ready to find the joy in anything, everything—like the ringing of small silver bells.

She was one of those girls who is capable of bringing sunshine into the darkest shadows.

She held nothing back, gave herself fully to the zest of living. Her appetites were swift to rise, and she slaked them with a joyous eagerness. She held nothing back, kept nothing in reserve.

When she made love, every ounce of that tiny body was thrown fully and passionately into the complete giving of herself. She did not merely allow Longarm to take her. She engulfed him. Contained him. Took all of his energies and captured them within herself.

Maddy Williams had been one of the most thoroughly delightful partners Longarm could recall knowing. Which was saying plenty.

That had been . . . what? Three years ago? No, not quite that long. Closer to two and a half. In the summer it was, and they had driven out on a picnic. Found a lush meadow high on a mountainside and made love under the clouds, and later, when they lay side by side with Maddy's hair spread over his shoulder like a silken cloak, a herd of elk came down through the glade, stepping with solemn dignity out of the screen of pale, trembling aspen and trooping in single file toward the creek far below, never once aware of the people who watched their passage.

That had been a wonderful moment, Longarm remembered. And afterward they made love again, and Maddy exclaimed over and over that day and for many days after about how magnificent the elk were and how beautiful.

He remembered that day now. And so much more.

There were many memories of Maddy.

Including memories of the screaming fury she displayed when he told her it was time that he had to return to Denver and to his responsibilities.

Quick as she was with joy and passion, she was also quick to anger, as he learned that day.

His final memory of her was the raw, bitter sound of her curses.

Until now.

"Been a long time, Maddy." He reached out to take her into his arms.

He drew her to him and hugged her. There was a moment of resistance. For several long seconds she felt wooden in his embrace, no more responsive than a softly padded oak plank might have been.

Then she made a small sound that seemed almost a

50

whimper, and after that she relaxed to his touch. Her arms came around him and she pressed her cheek against his chest.

She was so small she came only as high as his sternum, but there was so much energy in her that her size was easy to forget because there always seemed to be so much of her.

"Do you remember the elk?" he asked, his voice a whisper directed into the rich, red hair on the top of her head. He felt her nod in response. "I've never forgot that day," he told her.

"Me neither." She paused for a moment. "Do you want me, Custis?"

"You know I do, Maddy. You know I can't look at you without wanting you. Never could." He smiled and tipped her chin up so he could kiss her, then said, "Reckon I never will."

Her look was very serious for reasons he could not begin to guess at.

Then she nodded and, stepping back away from him, began to remove her clothes.

# Chapter 12

Maddy's body had changed some since Longarm last saw her naked. Her breasts were fuller, heavier somehow. Her nipples were larger and somewhat darker in color. And her belly, which used to be so unusually flat, was now rounded and slightly protruding, like the plump swell of a small melon.

She was still lovely to look at, though. Still so desirable she put a lump in Longarm's throat just from looking at her.

And an even larger lump in his jeans from wanting her.

She saw that and, with a small, almost sad smile, said, "Yes, I remember the elk, Custis. I remember that too." She gestured toward the erection that was fighting against the cloth that contained it. "We gave each other a lot of pleasure then, didn't we?"

"Aye, Maddy, I'd say we did, you an' me."

"Then let me please you again, Custis." She came to him and stood almost shyly before him while she reached down to caress and fondle the bulge behind his fly.

After a moment she sighed. And slowly sank to her knees. She pressed her face against him and he could feel the heat of her breath through the intervening layers of cloth.

She unbuttoned his fly and very gently disengaged his swollen erection from the nest of clothing that impeded him.

"This is every bit as handsome as I remember, Custis," she said.

Then she tickled the underslope of the gleaming red head with the tip of her tongue.

That slight contact was enough to tantalize and to tease, enough to make his pecker bounce and throb in response. He remembered that that had been one of the things she enjoyed, a real source of amusement for her. She liked to tease his prick and make it jump with every slight lick or dart of her constantly inquisitive tongue.

She did it again now, and then for some reason frowned as she closed her eyes and sucked his head and foreskin into the moist, sweet heat of her pretty mouth.

Longarm groaned aloud. The sensations Maddy Williams gave him were exquisite. She could please a man more completely than damn near anyone else he'd ever known.

But always before she'd done so with a bright and bubbly abandon. Tonight she was solemn and quiet.

She held him inside her mouth and ran her tongue round and round the head of his cock, all the while continuing to suck so that her cheeks hollowed with the force of it.

Longarm loved looking at her while she held him in her mouth like that. She had always been at her prettiest at those moments, he thought.

The sensations she was giving him mounted and quickly grew. She slipped one hand inside his fly to cup his balls on her palm while her fingertips went unerringly to that extraordinarily sensitive flat between the base of his scrotum and his asshole. She lightly tickled him there while she continued to suck hard on his cock.

The feeling was so grand that for a moment Longarm forgot where he was and almost lost his balance as his legs relaxed a bit too much. He reeled back on his heels, righted himself, and regained his balance.

When he rocked back like that he pulled free of Maddy's lips, and there was a loud, wet plop as the suction was broken.

Maddy reached up to grab Longarm's shaft and steady him so she could take him back into her mouth.

Longarm was smiling down at her, enjoying the curve of her eyelashes stark against her cheek when seen from that particularly pleasurable angle.

Then a gleam of light reflecting off a bit of jewelry caught his eye, and he gaped.

A spear of remorse shot through him and his erection subsided, shriveling away even though his pecker was still inside Maddy's sweet mouth.

"Custis? What's wrong, dear?"

"I didn't . . . Maddy, what the hell is that on your finger there?"

"Surely you know what a wedding band is, Custis."

"But . . . jeez, Maddy. I mean . . ."

She frowned. "You said you wanted me, didn't you?"

"I thought . . . I didn't know you'd married, Maddy."

"You didn't?"

"How the hell could I've known a thing like that?"

"I guess . . . I guess I thought you would have read about it in the newspapers. It was in the Denver papers. I know. I've seen some of them."

"Maddy, I don't know that the hell you're talking about."

"But I thought . . . I mean, I need a favor, Custis. I need the biggest favor anyone could ever ask of anybody else, and I guess I kind of thought that you wanted me to, you know, make it worth your while. Sort of."

She was still naked. Still on her knees before him. His prick, soft now and withdrawn inside his trousers, still was slick with her spit.

Longarm felt like the worst kind of son of a bitch.

First he'd gone and attacked her in the dark without warning.

And then he'd made her get down on her knees and demean herself even though she was a married woman.

Longarm turned away and hastily buttoned up and re-settled his clothing. He kept his back to her and said, "Put your clothes on, Maddy. Then we'll talk."

"Whatever you say, Custis. I will do . . . anything . . . to save my husband's life. I mean that, Custis. *Any*thing."

He didn't answer. Shit, he couldn't. Not without saying something that would make him seem even more the fool than he already felt.

# Chapter 13

They perched at opposite ends of one of the cots, the distance between them seeming much longer than it in truth was.

But then the distance between them now was very, very great so far as Longarm was concerned.

"When I saw you at the restaurant earlier today I thought . . . I couldn't help thinking that you came here for something to do with Gary. Then I talked to Tyler and he said no, I shouldn't get my hopes up. He'd just come back from seeing the governor and there wouldn't be any change. It will all . . ." She stopped, her voice breaking into choked-back sobs, then with great effort went on as if nothing had happened. "Monday," she said. "It will all proceed according to schedule at dawn on Monday."

Longarm kept his eyes averted from Maddy's discomfort. He pulled a cheroot from his pocket and concentrated on trimming and moistening and lighting it, trying to build the perfect coal while beside him a young woman wept.

"You know, Maddy," he said in a soft and gentle voice after several minutes had gone by, "I don't really understand what it is that you're trying to tell me about here."

"You haven't read about it in the newspapers? Really?"

"Read 'bout what, Maddy?"

"My husband, Custis. Gary Lee Bell."

"Him? Jeez, Maddy. How'd you get hooked up with somebody like him?"

Maddy looked Longarm square in the eye and in a much stronger voice said, "Just lucky, I guess, Custis. Just very, very lucky."

Gary Lee Bell, as anyone who'd read a newspaper over the past four or five months would likely know, was scheduled to hang soon—Monday morning according to Maddy, and she should damn sure know—after being convicted of murder.

Longarm remembered the notorious case fairly well. Bell was a drifter and ne'er-do-well. He'd shown up at a mine in the north of Wyoming Territory somewhere with a hard-luck story and a hand out. The miner had taken him in. At least that was what the newspapers said. What the papers implied was that there was a daughter involved too. Maddy, of course. The papers had made a great show of how circumspect and restrained they were being in refusing to give details of the relationship with the miner's daughter. At the same time they managed to imply all manner of sordid and unsavory possibilities. Then . . . Longarm's eyes widened a bit as it belatedly occurred to him that if Madelyn was involved in this story, so was her father.

"Damn, Maddy. I'm sorry about your pa. When I read the stories in the papers . . . Williams isn't that uncommon a name. I never thought about it being him."

"Everybody knew him as Windy most all his life, Custis. The newspapers used his real name of Rupert."

"Yeah, well, I'm mighty sorry for your loss. Your pa was a likable cuss. I always got along well with him." Longarm shook his head. "Most everybody did, I think."

In the newspaper accounts it was this Bell fellow's boss who'd turned up dead, first going missing, and then finally discovered at the bottom of a flooded prospect shaft. By then Bell had married the mine owner's daughter. And with her father gone, the mine and the girl both belonged exclusively to Gary Lee Bell.

Until, that is, a freak of circumstance disclosed the body and formal charges of murder were placed. There was a trial and conviction, an appeal . . . and now on Monday there would be an execution to put an end to it.

Except . . .

"Gary didn't do the things they said, Custis. I swear to you he didn't. I just . . . can't prove that he is innocent." She slid down the length of the bed until she was beside him, her body warm and close against his. She gripped his elbow in both her small hands. "I don't have much money, Custis, but I really will do anything to prove Gary's innocence. Anything, dear. And you can save him, Custis. I just know you can."

Her right hand left his elbow and nestled warm and inviting in his crotch.

# Chapter 14

Longarm bent and kissed Maddy very lightly on the forehead. With a sad smile he gently lifted her hand away from his body and placed it firmly into her own lap. "I'll be glad t' listen to anything you have to say, Maddy. But not because o' that. All right?"

Madelyn Williams Bell nibbled at her lower lip for a moment in thoughtful contemplation. Then she nodded and squared her shoulders. "Thank you, Custis. You're a dear friend."

"We'll see 'bout that, Maddy. We will see."

She patted his knee, not in invitation but as an acknowledgment of sorts, then left his side and crossed the tack room to the shelf where she had placed her clutch purse. She carried it back and sat, not so close to him this time, while she opened the bag and brought out a tattered scrap of paper.

The back of the single sheet bore a three-cent stamp and a crudely scrawled address directing the letter—for that was what it seemed to be—to "M. Bell, Takin Watter, W.T." The note had been folded and mailed without the formality of being enclosed within a separate envelope. Longarm was frankly amazed that it had ever reached Maddy.

If, that is, it really had. There was only a dark smear

59

where a postmark should have been, making it impossible for anyone to read where or when it was alleged to have been mailed.

In lettering just as crude as the address, the letter said: "Seen Windy Medcin Boz 2 daz gone. Live. Tell at." Few though the words were, their scrawl took up most of the sheet.

Longarm could get most of it easily enough. The letter—and it was not signed—purported to come from someone who claimed to have seen Windy Williams alive within two days of his mailing the letter. Whenever that might have been. Certainly, though, it was after Williams's body was discovered or the incident would not have been deemed noteworthy.

Windy Williams. Alive. "Tell at." It took Longarm a moment to work that out. Then he recalled that Sheriff Dillmore went by the initials A.T. Tell A.T. Tell the sheriff. Windy Williams was alive and therefore Gary Lee Bell could not have murdered him, should not hang by the neck until dead come the dawning Monday.

"Where'd you get this, Maddy?"

"I . . . is that important?"

He gave her a hard look. And waited for her to answer.

"Somebody left it at my house. Inside, on the table. I was out . . . I don't remember where, down inside the mine probably looking for a little high-grade I could turn into cash to pay Tyler with . . ."

"Excuse me, that's twice you've mentioned somebody named Tyler. Who is he?"

"Our lawyer. Tyler Overton. I owe him . . . I don't know how I will ever be able to pay him all of it. If I ever can."

"Sorry for the interruption. You were telling me about how you came by this letter."

"Yes. Like I said, I was out of the house. When I came in, the letter was lying on the table. I never saw who left it there. I suppose it was misdirected somehow and eventually someone realized where it was supposed to go and

60

just . . . brought it by as a kindness. Something like that.''

"But you didn't get it from the postmaster here like you normally would.''

"No. In fact I asked afterward if it had come to somebody else through the regular mail. He said he didn't remember seeing it before. Not that that necessarily means anything.''

"Why'd you ask him about it to begin with if you didn't think it was important?''

"Tyler said I should. He thought it could be important, I think.''

Longarm grunted. Tyler was right. "And this was how long ago?'' he asked.

"Last Thursday, I think.'' She paused, reflected, and then nodded firmly. "Yes, it was definitely on Thursday. I came into town Friday to let Tyler see the letter, but he was away. I saw him Saturday morning. That's when he told me to take the letter to Mr. Burnette, and we did. Tyler wanted to know as much as he could before he went down to Cheyenne to ask for the stay of execution. He went—I forget if it was Sunday or Monday that he left, Sunday I think—but he told me he wasn't really very hopeful. He felt he had to try, but he didn't think the letter would do much good. It didn't, of course. He gave it back to me this afternoon. He came back on the same stage you did, actually. That was why I was in town today, to see Tyler and see if he had good news for me.''

"So he's already taken the letter to Cheyenne and showed it to whoever needed t' see it?''

Maddy nodded. She sighed and looked off into a far corner of the small room, her thoughts and her gaze quite obviously going far beyond these confining walls. "Tyler said the courts wouldn't consider this to be evidence. Not without a signature or—I forget what he called it—something to back up what it says.'' She turned to look at Longarm. Her eyes were huge and moist, pleading. "You can make them listen, Custis. I know you can.''

"Not t' this, I can't. Your lawyer is right in what he told you about that. This paper here isn't anything close t' being the sort o' evidence that a court of law would need. And believe me, Maddy, it takes a heap o' proving before any court will back up an' reverse the decision of another. In order for this note t' do any good for your husband, Maddy, the court would pretty much have t' see your pa himself. Or at the very least see real proof that he's still alive. Not some note from somebody claiming to've seen Windy but Windy himself. Why, even if this letter is true—an' you can understand how anybody much less a judge would be skeptical when it's the condemned man's wife that claims to've found such a proof—but even if it's true, Maddy, the court would have t' think it could be a case o' simple mistaken identity. Just like what brought me here t' Talking Water now. We got a tip from a fella who honestly believed he'd seen a wanted man. Turned out to be somebody unlucky enough to look a whole lot like this murderer but innocent as could be. Well, this could be that same sorta deal. So no, I can't imagine a court agreeing to block an execution on the basis o' this here letter. I'm sorry, Maddy, but the only way a court or the governor is likely t' believe Gary Bell didn't kill your pa would be for somebody to produce your pa for them alive an' well."

"Then that is what you will have to do, Custis. Isn't it?"

"Pardon me?"

Maddy tossed her head and clamped her lips into a tight, thin line. "Why, you will simply have to go to the Medicine Bows and look for him. You know Daddy. If you find him you can take him to Cheyenne with you. You have to go past the Medicine Bow diggings and through Cheyenne to get back to Denver anyway. It wouldn't be all that much out of your way.

"And there is time enough. This is only Tuesday night. The execution isn't until Monday. There would be plenty of time for you to reach the discovery field in the Medicine Bows and just . . . you know . . . look around. You know

Daddy. He can't resist any new find or rumor of a find. He always has to see whatever is on the other side of the mountain. That's what has happened. I know it. He isn't dead. He just decided one evening to go someplace else. He's done that sort of thing before, you know. He always turns up eventually. But this time . . ."

"If you don't think your father is dead, Maddy, how d'you explain the body that was in that mine shaft?"

"It was in water, Custis, and all they recovered were some bones. Somebody decided it was Daddy because he's the only person who was missing from around here at the time. But it could have been anyone. Tyler argued in court that the skull was that of an Indian who probably fell into the shaft by accident. Tyler claims there is a way a scientist can look at the teeth on a skull and tell if the person was white or Indian. But we didn't have any scientists around here to testify about that, and we couldn't afford to send back East and hire one to come all this way. Tyler talked to the sheriff and the county commissioners about it, but they said they didn't have any money to waste on something like that, especially when they didn't believe it was true to begin with. The judge wouldn't even let Tyler tell the jury what he believed—about the teeth, I mean—because there wasn't any evidence to support what he said. Tyler read about it somewhere, you see, but he couldn't find the article again and couldn't remember exactly where he'd read it. So anyway, there was no evidence that the judge would accept and the jury never heard that argument. And that was the best defense Gary had. Tyler never got to say a word about it in court. Just in . . ." She frowned.

"Chambers," Longarm suggested.

"Yes, that was it. Tyler argued his point in chambers, but the judge ruled against us. The jury never heard any part of that."

Longarm gnawed on the end of his cheroot for a while before he said, "I don't s'pose it'd be possible for a person t' get a look at that skull after all this time, would it?"

"I . . . I'm sure I don't know, Custis. Why? Is it important?"

He frowned, then admitted, "Could be. You see, Maddy, I happen t' know that your lawyer is right. There is a way t' look at teeth an' tell if they belong to an Indian or to a white man."

"And if you see those teeth and know they couldn't be Daddy's, then you can get the hanging stopped?"

"Dammit, Maddy, I never said that. And don't you go getting your hopes up." But in truth it was what he was thinking. He just didn't want to tell the girl that. Not yet.

"The only reason people believed Gary killed Daddy, Custis, is because he'd gotten me in a family way and everyone knew Daddy was furious about it. That and because everyone thinks Gary wanted Daddy's gold mine." She snorted rather bitterly. "There isn't anything in that dirt hole worth a good argument much less a murder."

Longarm looked down at Maddy's belly.

"I know, I'm not that far along. Not with this one."

"I see. You got a kid tucked away someplace?"

"Yes. A little boy. I named him Gary Rupert in honor of my husband and my daddy."

"And this one . . . forgive me for mentionin' it, but hasn't your husband been in jail five, six months now?"

She blushed. And nodded.

"Is the territory o' Wyoming doing something different these days an' letting wives into prison cells?"

Maddy blushed again. Then with a sideways grin she shrugged and said, "You know me, Custis. It's something I've always enjoyed anyhow. I told you twice already that I'd do anything to help Gary, and I meant it. And I do owe Tyler an awful amount of money, more than Gary and me could ever hope to repay. I thought if it might help to get Gary out . . ." She shrugged again, but this time there was no grin to go along with it.

"I see. Sorry I brought it up." Longarm took a deep draw on his smoke and held it in his lungs for a bit before slowly allowing it to trickle out. He was more glad than ever that he'd asked Maddy to put her clothes back on. But for a much different reason now than at first. "I, uh, reckon I could take a look at that skull they found. If it's still around, that is. Just remember that there's no guarantees. We aren't dealing with rational, sane human persons here. We've dealing with a court o' law. And those two ain't the same. So before it gets any later, girl, let's us look up your Mr. Tyler . . . what'd you say his name is?"

"Overton."

"Yeah. Him." Longarm stood, the cartilage in his knee joints popping, and stubbed the butt of the cheroot out before leaving the tack room for the straw-littered barn area.

When they got outside, the night air seemed damn near balmy in spite of the thick, wet layer of snow that covered Talking Water and everything around it.

# Chapter 15

Maddy waited outside while Longarm went into the Five Aces—Longarm figured the owner of a place with a name like that either had a fine sense of humor or balls made of pure brass—and bought a bottle for the stage guard, George, and his driver pal, Jesse. Longarm owed them twice now, for the room and again for the privacy, and besides, he wanted to tell them it was safe to go back now if they were ready to turn in. The gift pleased them. Good bonded whiskey instead of the much cheaper popskull made from raw alcohol and floor sweepings. Or whatever. He accepted one drink with them, then excused himself.

"Sorry I took s' long," he said when he finally rejoined Maddy on the sidewalk.

"It's all right. I was enjoying the air. It feels so soft tonight. And the sound of the creek." She hugged herself and lifted her face toward the stars, bright now that the storm had passed. "I like it here. It's a place where I'd like to stay. We lived in a lot of camps, Daddy and me, but never in one place very long. Even when Daddy brought in a nice discovery, which wasn't very often, he'd just sell out and move along. The profits from any one strike were only used to look for another. That's one of the things— Custis, I know you won't believe me, considering what I have in my belly here, but I am very much in love with my husband. I truly would do anything to save him.''

''Even fake a note saying your father has been seen alive?''

She gave him a level, unflinching look and said, ''Yes, Custis, I would do that. I didn't. But you know that I would.''

He nodded, knowing it was the truth.

''You don't know Gary, Custis, but he is . . . wonderful. How can I explain it to you. He has rattled around as much as I have. Never a place to really call home. He was orphaned when he was little and passed around from one relative to another. Farmers, mostly. He says he came to hate farms. All the drudgery and effort and then the weather turns wrong or the locusts come or there is hail or no rain or too much rain or cold nights or days too hot. Always something wrong.''

Longarm said nothing, but the truth was that Gary Lee Bell's feelings on that subject were very much the same as Longarm's. He admired the stubborn, hopeful persistence that a farming man must have. But he'd long ago sworn that he would never again walk behind the ass end of a mule nor hang onto the handles of a moldboard plow.

''Later,'' Maddy went on, ''he went from one job to another. None of it meant anything to him. Those jobs were just ways to survive. Then . . . he came to work for Daddy, helping muck out the drift Daddy was working on. Gary isn't handsome, you know. Not the same way you are. But he's sweet. And so gentle. I can't tell you . . . when he looks at me, Custis, there is, like, almost like a light that's in his eyes. And a softness, all warm and tender. Just for me. Like I'm the only person in the whole world that's important to him. When he looks at me like that I get all squiggly and warm inside and I want to hold onto him and protect him. Does that sound funny? I mean, I know it's supposed to be the boy who protects the girl and all that. But whenever I look at Gary I want to be the one to hold him and keep him warm and safe. You know?"

He didn't. And didn't try to answer.

"Gary and me talked." She smiled, still looking up toward the stars. "Can you believe that? Me? Talking? Custis, you may not believe this either, but I think Gary and me talked more than we screwed. And you can believe we screwed plenty. I . . . I guess you'd say that I taught him how to do that. Oh, he'd been with whores sometimes. But he'd never had a regular girlfriend before. He didn't know much except to crawl on top and root around until something felt good." She laughed. "He's a good learner, though. I taught him plenty. Including some of the things you showed me back there in Telluride." She looked at Longarm. "Do you mind me telling you that?"

"No, I don't mind," he said gently. And discovered when he said it that it was true.

"One of the things we found out we both wanted was a home. A real home where we could stay in one place. Good times or bad we'd stay right there and see things through. I mean, that's what marriage is all about, isn't it? Seeing things through? Together?"

"Yeah. Yeah, Maddy, I suppose maybe that's true."

"I thought . . . until they charged Gary with murder, Custis, I thought I'd finally found everything I needed in this whole stinking world."

He was startled to see that despite the calm tone of her voice her cheeks were streaked with tear tracks. Apparently she had been weeping for quite some time now.

"Even after Daddy left—disappeared, I suppose I should say; everyone else certainly does—even after Daddy left I was really and truly happy for the first time in my whole life. I had Gary and we had our baby on the way, and we had the cabin to live in. We didn't have much money. Daddy never has been very good at picking claims. Just bad luck, I suppose. But that didn't matter. We didn't need much. A little color now and then . . . we worked the mine together, Custis. Just the two of us. I spun the drill and

68

Gary swung the singlejack, and we could take out enough to keep us in powder for tomorrow and flour for today. We didn't have to have anything more than that. And we had a *home*. Do you see, Custis? We had us a home, Gary and me. Then somebody found that dead Indian, and it all fell apart.''

Maddy shivered and, staring intently up at the stars while tears streamed down her face, added, ''God, Custis, I'm so scared I can't hardly stand it. I'm gonna lose Gary, and I love him so much. And even if the governor stays the execution I'm gonna lose him, Custis. He doesn't know about this baby that I'm carrying, and I can't tell him about it, I just can't. I can't let him go to the gallows for something he didn't do and . . . and with this haunting him too. How could I have been so *stupid*, Custis? Can you answer that one question for me? Can you?''

But of course he could not.

He was discovering, it seemed, that there was more to young Madelyn Bell than he'd thought.

And more than he'd really wanted to know.

Longarm reached for another cheroot and cleared his throat somewhat too loudly.

''Let's go see this Tyler Overton fellow an' see what he can tell me 'bout the skull they say is your pa's.''

# Chapter 16

There probably was not a "proper" house in the whole of Talking Water, but Lawyer Tyler Overton's came close to it. His home, while built of aspen like most of the structures, was meticulously pegged and chinked and—wonder of wonders—even painted. Well, whitewashed actually. But Longarm figured in a place like Talking Water whitewash ought to count as paint. The walls were that peculiarly flat, chalky finish common to whitewash, while the door and shutters had been painted—the real stuff this time—in some contrasting dark color. Since it was night, Longarm could not tell for sure just what color the trim was, but it looked mighty nice anyway.

Underneath each of the front-facing windows there was a dirt-filled flower box that still had the dry and barren remnants of last summer's flowers poking forlornly through a mantle of fresh snow.

All in all, Longarm was impressed with Maddy's lawyer.

Then the door was opened in response to Maddy's knock, and Longarm realized that it probably wasn't Tyler that he should be impressed by when it came to the amount of care that had been given to this remote homestead.

The door was opened by a young woman. A very visibly pregnant young woman actually.

Maddy was a few months along with Overton's baby. His wife looked to be damn near nine months gone with hers.

Tyler, it appeared, was a sure enough breeder. The man's judgment might be called into question but not his abilities.

"I hate to bother you so late, Doris, but could we speak with your husband, please?" Maddy was asking. "This gentleman is Deputy United States Marshal Custis Long, Doris. He thinks he may be able to help us with Gary's case, but he needs to speak with Tyler."

"Of course, Mrs. Bell. Please come in and have a seat. I'll tell Mr. Overton you are here."

Mrs. Bell. Mr. Overton. The lady of the house was formal. And timid. Her voice was thin and there was something—sadness? or was he only imagining that?—in it that made Longarm think Doris Overton was one of those plain and awkward women who would call their husbands "mister" even in the privacy of the bedroom.

Maddy went inside and helped herself to a seat. It was clear she was familiar with the place. Longarm took a little longer, carefully wiping his boots on a rag rug laid across the entryway and then removing his Stetson before stepping into the house. A primly unsmiling Mrs. Overton took his hat and hung it on a deerhorn rack secured to the front wall before she disappeared behind a blanket suspended over a doorway leading into the north end of the cabin. Longarm could hear a grunt and then a low and not particularly happy murmuring before finally there was the sound of feet hitting the floor and some creaking of springs. Lawyer Overton, it seemed, had been abed. And likely would have preferred to stay that way.

Several minutes passed before Overton made an appearance. When he did, however, he was fully dressed, to include vest and carefully knotted tie, although he had not put on his suit coat.

"Mrs. Bell," he said with a half bow in the direction of the young woman who was bearing his child. One of them.

71

Then he turned and extended a hand in Longarm's direction. He smiled hugely. And so believably that Longarm suspected this man would enter politics sooner or later. "Deputy Marshal Long. We meet again."

Tyler Overton was one of the two lawyers who had shared the stagecoach journey up from Bitter Creek, his colleague disembarking at McCarthy Falls and Overton continuing on here to Talking Water.

Longarm remembered him well enough, although they had hardly exchanged a half-dozen words on the long trip north.

Overton was not what Longarm might have expected for such a ladies' man. The lawyer was soft and plump and pink of complexion. He had an outsized rump, a massive belly, and was already going bald even though Longarm doubted he was more than thirty years of age if that old. He even managed somehow to give off an air of something approaching piety. As if he were the perfect model of virtue and circumspection. If he was not already the deacon of some church, then he damn well ought to be for he looked the part to perfection.

If any proof was ever needed that a man shouldn't be judged on the basis of appearance alone, then Tyler Overton could serve as a most wonderful example.

Still, every man is entitled to his own ways, and Longarm hadn't come here to make any rulings on the subject of the good counselor's morals. Hell, Longarm knew he wasn't in any position to pick up the first stone and fling it at this guy anyhow. So he smiled a friendly hello and shook the fat man's hand. "My pleasure," Longarm assured him, and Overton said pretty much the same in return as politeness dictated.

"My wife says you may have new information about the Gary Lee Bell case, Deputy?" Overton said, motioning Longarm to a place on the velveteen-covered settee that seemed to be the showpiece of the parlor furnishings.

"That isn't exactly correct," Longarm told him. "But

Maddy—I've known her and her daddy from some years back, you should understand—Maddy was telling me about the skull that was found and your theories concerning it. I was thinking at the very least I should take a look and see if the thing is the skull of a white man or an Indian. And why, now that I think about it, are you thinking it is an Indian's skull anyway?''

"To answer your last question first, sir, I theorize the skull is that of an aborigine largely because there are no white men missing from this area.''

Longarm raised an eyebrow.

"With the exception of Madelyn's father, that is. She assures me, you understand, that my client is blameless in this matter. Utterly innocent. And besides, there was a bear-claw necklace found in the same prospect hole as the body.''

"Anything linking the bear claws and the human remains?'' Longarm asked.

"Proximity, sir. Only proximity.''

"And I assume the judge didn't allow testimony about that either since he didn't allow you to talk about your skull theory.''

"Unfortunately true.''

"I'm sure you'll admit that your connection is mighty thin, Mr. Overton.''

"Of course I admit that. But I would have used it if I could have.''

Longarm nodded. There was nothing wrong with a lawyer using every scrap of evidence he could find on behalf of his client, no matter how far-fetched it really might be. And hell, what he claimed could even be so.

"But please, Deputy. You said you would like to see the skull itself? Do you mean to tell me that you actually know how to tell a white man's tooth from an Indian's?''

"Why, sure. Don't you? I mean, it's *your* legal defense we're talkin' about here,'' Longarm said.

Overton grinned and with a shake of his head admitted

73

that in plain fact, no, he had no idea which was which. "I am sure the article I read about the subject mentioned the differences. But that was a long time ago, sir, and I had no particular reason at the time to commit the facts to memory. It was merely something that stuck hazily in mind afterward and that I recalled when I was trying to put a defense together for Madelyn's husband. A possible way to raise reasonable doubt in the minds of the jurors, don't you see."

"So you really don't know yourself whether that skull belonged to a white or a red man?"

"I honestly believe it to have been the skull of an aborigine," Overton said solemnly. And shit, maybe he was telling the truth.

"But you don't know for sure," Longarm persisted.

"I do not know for sure," Overton affirmed. "Although we did try to find out. I made every attempt to ascertain the truth. On Gary Lee Bell's behalf I sent letters to the departments of anthropology and of medicine at Harvard, Emory, the University of Pennsylvania, the British Museum, and . . . can you think of any others, Madelyn?"

"Yale," she said. "I remember that we wrote to Yale. And didn't you ask the War Department to pose the question of their medical board also?"

"Yes, both of those, thank you." Overton looked at Longarm and shrugged. "We haven't had a response yet from any of them. I am afraid if we ever do hear anything it will be too late. Mr. Bell has only a few more days before his scheduled, um, demise."

"You still want to know?" Longarm asked.

"Oh, my, yes. If there is any possibility that I can find evidence to take to the governor, even up to the final seconds of life remaining to my client . . ."

"Then would you mind if I look at that skull for myself?"

"Sir, you tell me you possess the very information we have been so anxious to acquire. I would be delighted for you to view the skull. If only it were possible for you to do so before the execution date.''

Again Longarm's eyebrows went up in unspoken question.

''The skull and other remains have been buried, you see. They were held as evidence until the conclusion of the trial, then transferred to the state archives in Cheyenne, and when they were released from there they were offered to Madelyn for burial. They are, of course, officially presumed to be the mortal remains of her father, Rupert Williams.''

Longarm nodded.

''She quite naturally refused to take possession of them on the grounds that her father is still alive albeit missing.''

''Damn,'' Longarm mumbled, already seeing where this was headed.

''Exactly. So the state buried them in a potter's field outside Cheyenne. And to locate them again and exhume them would require a court order. God alone knows how long that would take, but I can assure you it could not be done before next Monday morning when Madelyn's husband is slated to die at the end of a hangman's rope.''

''That kinda looks like that then, don't it,'' Longarm said softly.

''I am loath to agree with you on the point, sir. But yes, I am afraid that that does indeed seem to be that.'' Overton spread his hands and, with an apologetic look in Maddy's direction, said, ''I am sorry, my dear, but I fear your deputy friend and I both have done quite as much as it is possible for us to do. The sad truth is that Gary will have to face his Maker next Monday morning.''

Maddy, Longarm saw, had begun very quietly to cry.

Dammit. He wished there'd been something he could have done about that.

He stood and extended his hand to Tyler Overton again. There was nothing Longarm knew of that he could fault the lawyer for. The man seemed to have given Gary Bell his very best. The problem was that there just wasn't evidence to support Overton's defense claims. And certainly

75

no evidence available to disprove the prosecution theories.

"Good night, sir," Longarm said, taking Maddy by the elbow and steering her toward Overton's front door. "Sorry we bothered you s' late."

"I only wish your visit had been a more successful one," Overton said. "Believe me."

"G'night," Longarm said again, and pulled the door open, letting a cool breeze sweep into the cozy parlor. He tugged his hat over his eyes and guided Maddy out onto the stoop.

# Chapter 17

Longarm snapped his fingers and, turning away from Madelyn, reached back and stopped Overton from closing the door behind them.

"Yes, Deputy?" Overton asked. "Is there something you forgot?"

"Y' might say that. It occurs t' me, sir, that you could tell me what the teeth on that skull looked like. I mean, since you don't know how t' tell the difference between an Indian and a white man, you wouldn't know how t' lie to me about it even if you was so inclined." Longarm smiled. "You see my point?"

"Yes, yes, I believe I do." Overton pursed his lips in deep thought, then motioned for Longarm and Maddy to return to the warmth of the house. "What is it you want me to describe, sir?"

"The back part o' the teeth. Not what you see when somebody smiles, like, but the back part that faces the tongue. What did that look like on the skull that was found?"

"Yes, I see. Mrs. Bell, you saw the teeth. Help me with this, would you? As I recollect them, the teeth on this skull were, um, how would one put it . . . concave. Is that the word I want? I can never remember which is which, concave or convex. One protrudes and the other dishes in.''

"An' which did these teeth do, Mr. Overton?"

"They dished inward. I would say that the backs of these teeth definitely dished inward, much like the hollowed scoop of a shovel. Would you agree with that, Mrs. Bell?"

"I really don't remember much about what they looked like, Tyler. I hated having to see that horrid thing and didn't look at it all that much."

"But would you say the teeth were concave or convex?" Overton persisted.

"I just don't remember well enough to say one way or the other," Maddy said, her voice showing a trace of annoyance at the second asking of the same question.

Overton turned to Longarm and shrugged. "My memory is definitely that the backs of the teeth were dished inward. Not a lot, mind. But most definitely inward."

"Concave," Longarm said.

"Is that it? Concave?"

"It's easier t' remember if you keep in mind that a cave is a hole that goes *into* the ground. Concave goes *in*, just like a cave."

"Ah, a mnemonic device. Thank you."

"A what?"

"Never mind, Deputy. But thank you. I'll not forget again which is concave and which convex."

"Yeah, if you say so."

"Ah, may I ask if the description has any meaning for you, sir?"

Longarm smiled. "Ayuh, I'd say that it does. What you just described t' me, Counselor, is the teeth of a dead Indian. No question about it. That skull they found couldn't have been that of Maddy's pa, Windy Williams. No way in hell that could've been so."

Maddy looked ready to shout for joy, and even Tyler Overton looked exceptionally pleased.

"In that case, sir, why, we have to report this to the judge. Or somebody. At once. They will have to stop the hanging. They will have to . . ." Overton's voice slowed and then died softly away.

"Yeah," Longarm said sadly.

"Custis? Tyler? What is it?" Maddy asked.

"The truth, my dear, is that unsubstantiated testimony, even that of a deputy marshal like our friend here, is unlikely to sway the opinion of a judge. In particular *our* judge. We already know his feelings in this area. And the governor—I doubt he would want to risk angering the political leaders of this entire end of the territory on the word of a mere deputy. Not when the local leaders are known to have firm friendships in Washington City. I am very much afraid, Mrs. Bell, that it would take something much more substantial than Deputy Long's inexpert opinion for the governor to conclude that your father continues in good health somewhere at an as yet unknown locale."

"That's true," Longarm agreed. "But . . . dammit, I ain't making no promises. We all know better than that. But Maddy, where'd you say that crazy letter o' yours came from?"

She opened her handbag and produced the tattered and much soiled slip of paper.

"You might not be able t' convince a judge or the territorial governor o' anything with your story about those teeth," Longarm said to Tyler, "but you've made a believer outa me. For whatever that's worth."

"Yes?"

"Maddy said it herself a little while ago. I gotta go right past the Medicine Bows on my way back t' Denver. It won't hurt nothing if I stop an' see if I can find my old friend Windy down there. The one thing that's absolutely guaranteed t' make the governor cancel that execution would be t' walk into the capitol building with Windy in tow." Longarm grinned. "You can't hardly have a murder if you don't have a victim, y'know."

"Custis, if you can save Gary . . ." Madelyn was weeping now, her face streaked with shiny tear tracks.

"I know. An' I'll do everything I can t' save him. You know that."

"Yes. Thank you."

"How do you intend to go about this, Deputy?" Overton asked.

Longarm shrugged. "Should be pretty simple. I'll head south on the coach tomorrow noon. If Windy is in the Medicine Bows he oughta be easy enough t' find. If I do find him I'll grab hold o' him an' take him to Cheyenne even if I gotta cuff and drag him. I can take him in as a material witness in a criminal case if nothing else. I don't need a writ for that. As a sworn officer o' the court, which technically I am, I can take him as far as the nearest federal magistrate on nothing more than my own say-so."

Overton nodded. "Are you familiar with the people and the politics of Cheyenne, sir?"

"Not particularly," Longarm admitted. "I've spent my share o' time there an' know some of the folks involved, but nothing stronger 'n that."

"Then may I make a suggestion?"

"I'll listen t' anything you want to say. No promises beyond that, but I'll surely listen," Longarm offered.

"I feel a strong moral obligation about this, Deputy. And I would not want anything to go wrong at the last moment. Would it be all right with you, sir, if I were to accompany you to look for Rupert Williams and, if that search is successful, ensure that the hanging is stopped?"

"It's fine by me, Counselor."

"And to tell you the truth, Long, I intend to make another appeal to the governor based on your testimony—or rather your knowledge—about those teeth even if the search for Rupert Williams proves fruitless. I know it will likely do no good. But I have to make the attempt. One way or another, sir, we simply *must* have that hanging canceled. I believed it before and now I know beyond doubt. Gary Lee Bell is an innocent man. If he hangs, our system of justice will be irreparably soiled. And I cannot permit that to happen, sir. I simply cannot.''

And damned if Tyler Overton didn't sound like he really meant it, Longarm silently conceded. Why, given a chance, Longarm might actually go and vote for the fellow if and when such a time were to come.

In the meantime, though, there was the little problem of finding Windy Williams and proving that Gary Lee Bell wasn't the murderer everyone believed him to be.

Longarm shook the fat lawyer's hand and once again bade him good night.

"I'll see you on the coach tomorrow, Counselor."

"So you shall, Deputy."

Longarm took Maddy by the elbow and led her out into the night and through the wet, ankle-deep slush that the recent snow was turning into.

# Chapter 18

Jesse, the stagecoach driver, dropped the mule's hoof with a loud groan and stood upright, arching his back and grimacing. Longarm understood quite well. There is nothing quite so likely to send darts of pain through a man's lower back as working on the feet of a horse or mule. The fool critters generally insist on putting their weight onto the man who is holding the foot, all the weight that would normally be on that foot and then some. It is a habit that seems to be bred into the four-footed bastards regardless of breed or training. All of them do it, and if there was a cure for it Longarm had never heard of it. A man's fortune would damn sure be assured if he could devise a way to train draft stock to quit leaning on people working with their feet.

That hadn't happened yet, though, so Jesse was stuck with the problem. He dropped that foot, sighed heavily, wiped off the hooked-shaped bit of wrought iron he was using for a hoof pick, and then bent to pick up yet another foot. Six mules. Twenty-four feet to keep cleaned and healthy. For without strong, healthy feet the most willing of mules isn't going to pull worth a damn. And it is the driver's responsibility to see to the welfare of his stock. No one else's.

Jesse laboriously completed the task of picking each hoof

so that it was free of impacted stones or pea gravel, then stepped back and allowed George and the Talking Water hostler to lead the harnessed mules into position and fasten them into the traces ready for the long downhill run—more or less—to distant Bitter Creek.

Longarm waited until the last moment, then tossed the butt of a cheroot aside and climbed into the stagecoach with a bare nod in Madelyn Williams Bell's direction.

The simple truth of the matter was that he was feeling downright embarrassed with the situation on the loading platform.

The thing was, Maddy was there to see them off. And so was Mrs. Overton. And there old Tyler stood, saying good-bye to two different women, each of whom was carrying his kid in her belly. And, well, Longarm sure as hell didn't consider himself any kind of a prude. But this was more than he was prepared for.

Fortunately he didn't have to say much of anything himself, if only because there was no point in trying to talk. Talking Water was more than living up to its name at the moment. The sound of the water cascading over the rocks in the nearby creek was so loud it was almost impossible to hear anything shy of a deliberate roar.

Which, mercifully enough, saved Longarm from having to come up with words that he didn't particularly want to say.

And besides, Maddy knew he would do his best for her presumably innocent husband. He'd already told her he would do that. Anything more would just be so much extra shit added to a pile that was already in place, so why bother.

Over on the platform Longarm could see Tyler Overton shaking Maddy's hand—acting oh, so proper and dignified while he did it—and then giving his mousy little wife a peck on the cheek in farewell.

It was a wonder half the womenfolk of Talking Water weren't lined up waiting for the fat lawyer to give them a good-bye grope.

But then that wasn't being entirely fair, was it, Longarm admitted silently to himself. After all, he didn't know the whole of the story here. Didn't know who'd first suggested what. Or what all might lie behind a moment's lapse . . . or a lifetime of deliberate lapses. That was the point. He just didn't know. And really shouldn't ought to judge. Longarm gave himself a stern reminder to that effect and looked away.

A moment later he felt the coach sag on that side as a passenger's weight was added, and Overton settled onto the middle seat beside Longarm, giving out a loud grunt from the effort of climbing into the vehicle. The man was damn sure out of shape if a couple of simple steps could cause him that much discomfort.

Longarm shifted over a fraction of an inch to give Overton a touch more sitting room. The coach tilted and swayed once more as another couple of passengers came aboard.

Overton obviously knew the men, nodding to them and speaking to them by name. Whatever the names were, Longarm couldn't catch them due to the loud chatter of the creek.

Slowly the coach filled with southbound passengers—all male, Longarm noted with no particular pleasure—while outside Maddy and Doris Overton dutifully waited to wave good-bye.

Finally George climbed onto the driving box and made sure the brake was set, while Jesse made a last-minute walk-around to make sure all was to his liking, then picked up the hitch weight that had been clipped to the off leader's bit ring. He wiped the muddy iron weight with a scrap of coarse sackcloth, and tossed the weight and leather hitch line into the boot at the back of the coach.

Jesse shouted something to the Talking Water agent, and with a grin and a wave climbed onto the box beside George.

Longarm heard the rifle-shot crack of Jesse's whip cut

through the babble of water noises, and the Concord lurched into motion.

Overnight to Bitter Creek, Longarm figured, then a short train trip east. Jog down to the new Medicine Bow diggings. And with any kind of luck they'd be able to find Windy Williams and prove Maddy's husband an innocent man in time to avert the hanging that was to take place first thing Monday morning.

Piece of cake, Longarm thought.

But then, how was a man to know?

# Chapter 19

By the time they got to McCarthy Falls that evening there was no remaining trace of the heavy snow that had fallen so recently. The day had been so warm that even the shadowed north faces of the mountainsides were melted clean, nothing but brown dirt, green fir, and gray rock showing where there had been a blanket of near-solid white just that morning.

"I was afraid there'd be drifts to block the way," one of the other passengers observed as he climbed down from the coach and stretched his legs. "Reckon now that Goshen Pass is behind we can count on easy running the rest of the way."

Jesse gave the man a dark look and opened his mouth as if to respond, then clamped his jaw shut as he thought better of whatever he might have said. The coach driver bent and once again began the laborious task of cleaning each of twenty-four hoofs.

George handed down luggage for one of the three men who were leaving the coach at McCarthy Falls, and secured the bags of two women who were boarding there.

Longarm was surprised to see that these were the same two ladies—he used the term as a matter of politeness, not description—who had ridden with him from Bitter Creek on the upbound journey just the day before. It seemed that they too were making the same quick turnaround that Longarm and Tyler Overton were.

"Everything all right?" Longarm asked Jesse as he offered the driver a cheroot and held a match to light both smokes, then handed a third cigar up to George.

Again Jesse opened his mouth, hesitated, and decided not to venture any guesses. "We'll see," was as far as the stagecoach jehu would commit himself.

There was time enough, but barely, for the through passengers to piss and maybe buy a dry sandwich from one of the butcher boys who were on hand in search of a sale. The coach was ready to roll out again before Longarm had time to finish his cheroot. He leaned in the doorway to ask the women if they would mind if he brought a cigar aboard with him, but like Jesse, decided to let the speech die unborn after he saw the venomous look one of the women was sending his way.

He settled for clearing his throat and stepping back to suck in a few quick, deep drags before he threw the half-smoked cigar aside—damn, but it hurt his feelings to have to do that—and was the last passenger to return to the coach.

The big Concord, several tons of wood and iron and vulnerable flesh, lurched and jolted and began a sickening sideways slide that brought a leap of discomfort into the pit of Longarm's stomach and sent several of the dozing passengers tumbling onto the floor.

"Whoa, goddammit, whoa," Jesse shouted. Not that there was much of anything the mules could do about the slide.

Longarm grabbed hold of the arm of one of the women to keep her from landing on the floor atop a salesman of medicinal products. Which earned him a grunt of thanks from the woman and a glance of sharp annoyance from the salesman, who obviously wouldn't have minded having the lady on top.

The coach wheels hit something solid and rebounded sharply back the other way, the sudden change of direction accompanied by the sound of wood splintering.

"Ah, shit, dammit, whoa," Jesse moaned loudly into the night.

The coach lurched again, slithered back and forth like a gigantic dog shaking its tail, and then finally came to a rocking stop on its creaking thoroughbraces.

"Jesus Christ," Jesse said.

"I wisht he wouldn't talk like that," one of the passengers complained. "He'll bring the wrath down on us."

"I don't think he was cussing," one of the whores suggested. "I think he was praying."

"What I think," Longarm said, "is that we all better get out and see if we're needed for anything."

Lawyer Overton was the first one out the door. He stepped down to the ground.

And promptly disappeared.

"Damn!" he yelped.

"What's the matter?"

"Be careful when you step down. Hang onto something." There was a low grunt and Overton's voice was strained. "It's slick as snot on ice out here. Mud. My feet went right out from under me soon as I stepped on the ground."

It helped that someone, either George or Jesse, scratched a match afire and lighted a lantern that he hung from one of the side curtain hooks above the window.

Tyler Overton's suit was liberally smeared with bright red mud, Longarm could see by the light of the lantern. So were the lawyer's hands. Obviously he hadn't thought before he'd tried to brush himself off. It looked like the only thing he had accomplished was to rearrange the mud into broader smears that covered most of his back and butt and right side. Longarm managed to keep from chuckling, mostly because he knew he could end up looking just as grimy if he wasn't careful when he got out of the coach himself.

"You gents go ahead," the woman nearer the door said as she pulled back and resumed her seat. "I ain't moving. You, Ada?"

"I didn't lose nothing out there, honey."

Longarm stepped down—*very* carefully—and immediately reached for a cheroot.

George produced a second lantern and climbed down. Jesse was already on the ground fussing with his mules, soothing them with soft mumblings and going from one mule to the next while he scratched their polls and rubbed the sensitive hollows beneath their jawbones. He did seem fond of those animals.

"Shit," George grumbled.

The lantern light showed the cause of the comment. The coach had skidded off the crown of the road—they were long since out of the mountains and traveling across the broad expanse of sage flats here—and managed to bang sideways into an old rut in the road. It wasn't even a rock that had done them in; there wasn't anything that solid in sight, just a narrow, mud-filled rut.

That rut had been quite good enough to cause a problem, though. The left rear wheel had two broken spokes.

"Shit," Jesse echoed when he finished calming his mules and came back to see to the trouble on his coach.

"Do we have a spare?" the medicinals salesman asked.

"Did your mama change your diddies for you?" Jesse snapped back, his voice testy.

"Damned if I can remember," the salesman shot back with a grin, not at all put off by the driver's annoyance. "Did yours?"

"No, and I think maybe that's why I got the red-ass now," Jesse said, conceding defeat pleasantly enough. "Anyway, yeah, of course we got spares. A couple of 'em. We also have a bitch of a deal to make the change."

That was true enough. It was night. In the middle of absolutely nowhere. And the ground here seemed to be solid mud. Cold as a witch's tit but gooey, gummy, slick, and slippery mud nonetheless.

And some poor sonuvabitch was going to have to crawl underneath the coach in order to set the screw jack—and somehow find a way to keep the damn thing from sinking into the muck once weight was applied—so they could get the busted wheel off and a new one bolted on.

Longarm puffed on his cheroot and kind of faded off behind the coach where he wouldn't be noticed if Jesse commenced to looking for volunteers. Like that whore had said when it came to getting out of the coach, he hadn't lost anything underneath the son of a bitch and there was nothing down there that he was going to go look for.

This was, he was beginning to suspect, gonna be a very long night.

# Chapter 20

"Screw it. I don't care. They're nothing but a coupla whores. They can pull their own weight or get out. That's what I say."

The other men gave the salesman—his name was Leonard—an uneasy glance. But it was apparent that they had been thinking pretty much along those same lines.

It was past dawn now and they still hadn't reached Howard Burdick's relay station.

Every man, Wind River employee and passenger alike, was pretty well plastered over with thick, caked mud. And if he could judge by the way he felt himself, Longarm thought, everyone was pretty near to the end of the line when it came to strength and stamina too.

Ever since hitting the flats the mud had gotten worse and worse until it was just plain impossible.

Cold, wet, clinging, slippery mud.

The mules were covered with it. The coach wheels were constantly mired in it. And the only way to move on was for everyone—everyone except the women, that is—to get out and push the heavy Concord coach out of the latest mud hole and onto whatever passed for solid ground.

There were places where they had to push—throw their shoulders against the coach body, grab hold of a wheel spoke and lift, take a grip on whatever was within reach and pull—a hundred yards and more at a time.

At this point it felt like they weren't so much riding in the stagecoach as they were having to pick it up and carry the damn thing to Burdick's.

Burdick's relay stop, Longarm thought. Funny how on the way north he had stopped there and had a better than merely decent bowl of stew and gone on again without ever once thinking to inquire about the name of the place or the owner or anything else about it.

Now, after a full night of shared labor, he knew the name and at least a partial personal history of every other bastard aboard, and was almost desperately interested in getting to Howard Burdick's no-longer-taken-for-granted relay point.

By now Longarm ached in every joint and every limb. He was winded and weary. His eyes burned and his legs ached from dragging around half a hundredweight—well, it *felt* like that much anyway, and who the hell was gonna produce a set of scales and dispute him if he wanted to make the claim—of cold mud that caked his lower legs to the knees.

That came from wading through the slimy shit every time the coach bogged down. And from slipping and falling every couple of minutes. There wasn't any way to avoid going down. Every man among them now looked worse than Tyler Overton had after that first experience long miles and hours back.

"Let the bitches help push. Their shit stinks just the same as ours does," Leonard Grohle complained.

"Jesse, what d'you say?"

"Hold it," Longarm put in. "You're just tired and feeling out of sorts, Leonard. We all are. But we aren't gonna fall so low as to make a lady get out and push a mud-bogged stagecoach. Now we just aren't gonna do such a thing as that."

"They ain't no damn ladies, Long. That's the point," Delmer Jelk said, siding with Grohle.

"All right then. Women. Same thing in my book. A man don't do that to a woman. Right is right, boys, even out here."

"I say we take a vote on it," Leonard said.

There was little doubt which way a vote would go. Longarm suspected Jesse and George would vote with him to let the women keep their seats inside the coach—they would pretty much have to or face trouble from their employer when they finally did reach Bitter Creek—but all the other men would likely vote to make the women labor.

Except for Overton? Longarm wondered. And honestly was not sure how the fat lawyer would cast a ballot. Either way . . .

"Boys, you can vote all you damn want. But I'm telling you this. I won't stand by and see anybody abuse a lady." He quickly held his hand up to stop the snorts of protest. "Woman, all right? If not ladies exactly, then women. We c'n all agree on that."

"Lady, woman, what the hell does it matter. Their legs ain't broke. They can help push."

"I reckon they could," Longarm agreed, "but they ain't going to. They're gonna stay right where they are. The man that tries to make 'em do otherwise, or who tries to put them out into this mud, is gonna get the crap knocked out of him." He grinned. "And let me tell you, fellas, having to do that would piss me off something awful, 'cause I'm already so tired I can't hardly fart without it putting me on my knees."

"You'd punch a white man to keep some whore from having to help out?" Jelk asked.

"I said it, Delmer. I'd damn sure do it. But hell, you go ahead an' do what you like. You know what your teeth are worth to you. Spend 'em if you feel the need strong enough."

"I don't think I want to fight about it." He too managed a grin. "Right now I'm not sure I could lift a fist to hit back at you if you stood still and gave me five minutes to wind up for it.''

''Look, I tell you what. I got''—he reached into his coat pocket and counted—''I got three cigars left here. Let's divvy them up and have us a break before we go at 'er again.''

''If it makes you fellas feel any better,'' George put in, ''you can all look yander. You see that smoke? That's coming from Howard's chimney. That smoke is cooking our breakfast, boys. And I for one want to get over there and wrap myself around it.''

There was a general lessening of misery among the men at the thought of hot coffee, piles of buckwheat flapjacks, and thick slabs of bacon.

Even more important, though, there would be an opportunity for everyone to scrape themselves free of mud, wash up, and just plain sit in comfort for a spell.

Lordy, but it had been one long, miserable son of a bitch of a night.

And close enough to see in these conditions probably meant they were still several hours away from reaching the relay station.

Longarm broke his cheroots in two and handed the pieces out among the men, saving a stub for himself. He sure as hell hoped Howard Burdick had some decent replacements on hand at that relay station, because the trip was only half over and Longarm would hate like hell to have to go the rest of this entire day without a smoke.

# Chapter 21

"Son of a bitchin' chinook," Jesse complained.

"Who?" Delmer asked.

Longarm, laboring at the mud-slimy wheel beside the salesman, gladly accepted an excuse for a moment's respite—any excuse would have been good enough—and paused to wipe cold, greasy sweat from his face while he explained. "Chinook," Longarm said. "It ain't a who, it's a what. A wind, actually. Warm wind. Gener'ly comes outa the west. And gener'ly is welcome because it cuts the cold and warms things up when you don't expect warmth. This time, though, comin' in behind a wet an' heavy snow, it's caused a helluva lot more trouble than the warm weather is worth. It melted all that snow like tryin' to wrap a ball o' butter round a stick and roast it over a fire. Melted it clean away. And o' course left all that water behind where the snow had been. That's why we got the mud now. Normal spring melt, see, happens over weeks or even months as things warm up a bit at a time an' most o' the water evaporates clean away into the air. The rest is runoff that swells the creeks and the rivers down low. Well, this time there wasn't no evaporation, not time enough for it, and there's too much water to run off in the regular way. Up in the mountains the creeks are busting their banks. Count on it. Out here on the flats there's no creeks to carry the runoff water. Out here what there is is mud.'' Longarm grinned. ''Or ain't you noticed?''

Delmer Jelk sighed, wiped a cheek that was already so grimy and mud-smeared that it was impossible to tell if he'd gotten it any cleaner or not, and took a fresh grip on the spokes of the wheel they were wrestling. ''Ready?''

''Ayuh, if you are.''

''On three then. One, two . . .''

''Jesus God,'' George moaned. ''I never been so tired in all my life.'' Even his voice seemed limp as he slumped to a sitting position on the hard and no doubt uncomfortable edge of the metal step into the coach.

They had been trying for twenty minutes or more to manhandle the big Concord—the miserable thing weighed more than three tons, and that was without adding the weight of all the mud that adhered to the undercarriage—out of this latest bog.

At this point even the mules were of little help. They too were exhausted, and unlike a horse that can be driven until it quite literally lies down and dies from excessive fatigue, a mule can be forced only so far. Then it will balk and refuse more work regardless of whips or prods. A mule will not allow itself to be worked beyond its capacity, although that capacity is enormous and rarely reached.

This time they had managed to reach the physical limits of all but two of Jesse's team, and two mules and a handful of weary men were not close to being enough to drag the massive stagecoach out of this bog.

What was most painful about it was that they were so tantalizingly close to their destination. They could see Howard Burdick's station less than a quarter mile off.

The way Longarm felt at the moment, though, that distance might as well have been a quarter of the continent as a quarter of a mile.

''Look, folks,'' Jesse said, leaving his mules and stum-

96

bling back to the side of the coach. "We aren't doing any good here. What we need is a little time for the chinook to dry out this mud or else a good freeze to firm up the ground. It's close enough we can all walk the rest of the way to Burdick's. We'll put the ladies on the backs of the two mules that are still pulling, and we'll walk in. Me and George can come back out when the ground has dried some or else tonight if we get a freeze. Any of you needs your bags or anything out of them, help yourself. Just remember you got carry it yourself. George, you carry the ladies' small bags for them. I'll take care of the stock."

"If you like," Longarm said, "I'll lead one of those mules that'll be carrying a lady."

"I'll take the other," Tyler Overton volunteered.

"Thanks, gents." Jesse had the appearance of a man who had just suffered a crushing personal defeat. But then, for the proud jehu of a Concord and six-up—and there were few men prouder than the flamboyant stagecoach drivers of the wide-open West—this failure to bring his coach in was indeed a crushing and a very personal form of defeat.

The rest of them had no regrets, though. Moving slowly, their limbs turned leaden from fatigue and their minds numbed by exhaustion, the menfolk left the bogged coach where it was and began a slogging trek through shin-deep mud to reach the comforts of Burdick's.

# Chapter 22

Heaven was a basin of warm water. And here Longarm had gone and found it right here on earth.

When the exhausted travelers arrived they discovered that Howard Burdick and his wife Jean had long since seen their predicament and were prepared to greet them.

Shoes and stockings were left at the front door, where the station host personally washed them in a huge laundry tub and set them aside to dry. While Howard was doing that, Jean was cheerfully issuing pots and small basins of warm water along with squares of soft, dry ticking to serve as towels so the guests could wash their feet and get comfortable again for the first time in many hours.

The ladies—well, so to speak—were given water and towels and sent off into the privacy of the Burdick's own sleeping quarters so they would not have to bare their limbs in front of the gentlemen. This despite the unacknowledged likelihood that any or all of the males present could well have screwed one of both of the female passengers.

But then, that was a part of what passed for moral propriety at the time and place. It was acceptable for a man to poke his pecker into a woman's snatch, but it would have been scandalous for him to look at her naked ankle in a public setting.

"We have coffee on the stove, folks, and breakfast will be on the table soon as you've all had a chance to wash up. Ham, hominy, and my good wife's biscuits and no need to hold back. There will be plenty enough for all. Over there by the settee is a box with some carpet slippers in it. Not enough for everyone, but help yourselves as long as they hold out. Anyone who has to go outside to the backhouse, don't try and put your shoes or boots back on; they'd just get muddy again. I have some gum rubber overshoes you can use. Just step into them on your way out. They're big enough it'll be like trying to wear a bucket on each foot, but at that it's better than getting cold and wet all over again. Keep your feet dry, gents, and you'll be all right. Get too wet and cold and you'll catch your death. And we can't have that, after all. The coach line needs all the paying passengers it can get, and so do we." Burdick was a slender, bespectacled man of middle years and sunny disposition. He had a bald patch on the crown of his graying head and a pencil-thin mustache. Longarm found the contract station keeper to be a thoroughly likable fellow. And an efficient sort as well.

Jesse was the last man in, having taken time to put his beloved mules to "bed" before seeking comfort for himself.

"Any news from down south, Howard?" Jesse asked.

"Nope. Not a whisper. Of course I don't have a telegraph point here. As for the northbound coach, I haven't seen anything of them yet. They're even worse overdue now than you were. Should have passed through here last night, but they never did."

"No, I seen that. They would've passed us on the road if they'd gotten here. You think they ever left Bitter Creek?"

Burdick shrugged. "Your guess is every bit as good as mine, Jesse."

The jehu frowned. "Damn road must be as bad to the

south as it is here. If that's so, we could be stuck here for days."

Longarm gave Tyler Overton a worried look. When they'd left Talking Water they'd thought they were in plenty of time to block the execution of an innocent man. But if they were to be stuck in the mud—literally so—for days here at this isolated outpost . . .

"When the northbound gets here, if the northbound gets here, we'll find out what the conditions are to the south," Jesse went on. "But hell, we're a long ways from getting our own coach the rest of the way in here to the station, much less heading south again. We'll just have to wait an' see how she goes."

From the back of the big public room came the sound of a cowbell clattering. "Breakfast, everyone," Jean Burdick called cheerfully. "Come and get something warm in your bellies before I throw it to the hogs." Then she laughed. And no wonder. There probably was not a hog, not a living one anyway, within eighty miles.

Longarm shrugged and, putting aside the problems of immediate transportation, followed his nose to the source of the tantalizing odors coming from the long trestle tables at the back of the place.

# Chapter 23

"Aw, hell," George moaned.

"What's the matter? Apart from the obvious, that is."

"We was hoping maybe things weren't so bad south of here? Well, forget that. Here comes the folks from the northbound. They're on foot and look more wore out than we was when we got here."

Everyone crowded to the door and two tiny windows at the front of the stage station. The view was not encouraging. Seven men and a woman were slipping and sliding their weary way through the gooey gumbo south of Burdick's. The men wore the bright, reddish-brown tint of mud to their knees or higher, and several of them looked like they had virtually bathed in the sticky stuff.

The whole thing would have been laughable under other circumstances, Longarm thought.

But not when an innocent man's life might be forfeit because of this aberration of nature.

"We'd best put more water in the stew, Ma," Burdick said to his wife with a wink. She immediately began peeling potatoes and slicing carrots while her husband pulled on a pair of rubber boots and went out to the old dugout that now served as a root cellar. And a cold locker for meats as well, as was attested by the slab of beef—or it might have been elk—that he soon brought back to chop into man-sized bites and add to the stew pot.

The situation here was not pleasant in many ways, but they were not going to starve while partaking of the hospitality of Howard and Jean Burdick, Longarm thought.

It took nearly an hour for the party from the northbound coach to reach the station.

And when they did Jesse was hopping mad.

"Damn you, Roy, where's your stock? Where's your mules?"

Roy, much older than Jesse and presumably senior to him with the Wind River line, shrugged and looked away, avoiding the fury that flushed Jesse's face a dark, mottled purple.

"You left them back there, didn't you?" Jesse accused.

"Dammit, Jess, they're mired s' deep we wouldn't never of got them loose an' all the way here. Shit, they're all right. They'll work theyselfs free an' graze whatever they can find close by. It ain't like they'll go far. Not in this shit, they won't. They'll be right there when we need 'em again."

"The hell they will," Jesse declared. "You and Charlie are going back there. Right damn now. You're gonna go back and get those mules and bring them in here to where they can have some shelter and fodder and dry feet. And you're gonna do it before you set down or have yourselves a bite to eat, either one of you."

"Aw, Jess . . ."

"Goddammit, Roy, you heard me. Right now."

"Who d'you think you are t' be giving me orders, Jesse?"

"I'll tell you who I am, Roy. I'm the son of a bitch that's going to beat hell out of you if you don't see to the welfare of your stock, that's who I am. I'm going to do that if I have to pick up a singletree and beat on you with it. And I don't figure to stop until those mules have been taken care of. You got that, Roy? Is it clear to you?"

"You got no right."

"I got whatever rights I'm willing to take, Roy."

"I'll see you lose your job over this, Jesse."

"You do that, Roy. If the boss wants to fire me for worrying about the stock and the passengers, that's fine by me. I wouldn't want to work for no line that won't care for its stock anyhow. Until then, though, you are gonna do what I told you or I will personally bust your jaw and do my level best to break every tooth in your head."

"Me and Charlie can't get six mules through all this mud. Not by ourselfs we cain't." There was a hint of a whine in Roy's voice now.

"Fine. Me and George will go along and help bring them in," Jesse declared.

Longarm sighed. Four men. Six mules. What the hell. "I'll go too," he said softly.

"Me too, dammit," Leonard Grohle mumbled. The expression on his face said that the offer surprised him as much as it did Longarm. "Well, we aren't any of us going to get out of here unless there's mules to pull both coaches, right?" he added, almost as if he felt a need to apologize, or at the very least to explain, for volunteering.

The argument was not particularly sound, of course. There were, after all, fresh mules out in the barn, Burdick's being a relay station and not merely a rest point. Not that Longarm intended to point that out to Grohle, who probably needed little encouragement to back out of his offer to help.

"Do we have rubber boots enough to go around?" Longarm asked.

"Plenty enough," Howard Burdick responded.

"Then bring out the rest of them, Howard," Jesse instructed. "We don't want to leave those poor animals stranded any longer than we have to."

Even so, it was mid-afternoon before the "rescue" party stumbled back to the security of Burdick's with the northbound team.

Men and mules alike were liberally coated with mud, and

Longarm doubted he'd ever been so completely worn out in all his life.

Jesse was happy—the only one of the six men who was—and busied himself with giving orders to Roy and Charlie about how the mules should be cleaned up and tended to once they were safe in the big, low-roofed barn.

Inside the station the southbound group had had a chance to become acquainted with the northbound passengers and all were mingling together. Longarm felt almost like a stranger intruding on someone else's soiree. He knew the people who had been with him on the southbound coach, but the newcomers were all completely unknown to him, though they now were relaxing in perfect comfort and companionship with the southbound crowd. He definitely felt a little left out.

Apart from the stagecoach crew, with whom Longarm was by now certainly familiar—albeit not particularly impressed—the new group included two men who might have been engineers or surveyors, a burly, hulking brute of a fellow, one slightly built dandy who had somehow made it through that sea of muck while carrying a fancy malacca cane with a brass mallard-head grip, a man who looked more cowhand than miner, and a woman whose veil kept Longarm from forming any opinion about her based on outward appearances. All he could tell about her was that her traveling gown was a dark, royal blue velveteen with a wide-brimmed hat to match. And of course the veil, very plain and very dark and imparting an aura of some mystery to her presence.

"Who's the lady?" Longarm whispered to the northbound shotgun messenger, Charlie, who seemed at least slightly more agreeable than his driver friend Roy.

"Damn if I know," Charlie returned without bothering to moderate his voice in the slightest. "Ain't seen nothing of her but that veil. Huh! She didn't even show no ankle when she got in an' outa the coach, so I figure she must be a sure 'nuff lady. Hoors don't keer an' regular women don't know how t' keep covered up that good. Takes a regular lady t' get in an' out a Concord an' not give a fella at least a little somethin' t' look at.''

The words were loud enough for everyone in the place to overhear. Including the woman in the blue gown.

Longarm felt an impulse to look for something he could crawl under. Something real low would have worked just fine.

"Thank you," he said dryly.

"Any time," Charlie responded, Longarm's tone passing him by completely.

"Marshal Long," Howard Burdick called out from the back of the big room. "Come have some coffee. It will make you feel better."

"Yeah, thanks. Thanks a lot, Howard." He walked far wide of the woman in blue on his way to join Burdick. And was pleased to see that the cheerful station keeper had a little something to sweeten the coffee. Something that came in a silver flask and tasted a damn sight better than common bar whiskey would have.

# Chapter 24

"Supper. Everyone come to the table now, and don't be shy. We have plenty enough to eat, folks," Jean Burdick called out, precipitating a slow and sluggardly drift toward the back of the huge common room.

Longarm, who had been sitting at the front of the station where a little fresh air came through the open door and windows—an indication that the chinook was still very much in effect here; otherwise that breeze would have been chilling rather than pleasant—held back. He had washed up earlier, but still felt gritty after practically bathing in mud and muck twice today. And besides that, he felt a growing urge to take a good, hearty crap. Eating a big meal when he already had to go did not seem a particularly good idea. So instead of joining the others, he slipped his feet into a pair of oversized gum rubber boots and went outside.

There was a rack containing four enameled steel washbasins along the south wall of the building, each with a small pot of soft soap beside it and each with a laundered feed sack hung nearby to serve as a towel.

First, though, he needed to visit the backhouse.

There were a pair of them actually. A two-holer for the gents and a much smaller shitter for the ladies. But then women passing through the station would be relatively rare and there wouldn't be so much need to accommodate them.

The last glow of sunset was fading behind the jagged ridges to the west as Longarm stepped inside the outhouse and let the door slap closed behind him.

Never one to make assumptions he took a moment to strike a match and check the surroundings before he dropped his britches and sat. Lucky that he did too, for some inconsiderate bastard had pissed all over the seat . . . and recently enough that the wood was still soaking wet. Perching on someone else's cold, wet urine was not Longarm's notion of comfort, so he shifted over to the seldom-used second seat off to the side, where it was a long and awkward reach to the paper bin but where things looked considerably cleaner.

No sense wasting a perfectly good match, so he lit up a cheroot and settled in for that most relaxing of life's tiny pleasures, a nice dump.

Smoke wreathed his head in the stagnant air inside the backhouse, and the heavy but not altogether unpleasant odor of a clean and well-limed outhouse added to his sense of well-being.

Yawning, he finished his principal mission and leaned over to take a handful of the crumpled scrap paper that had been provided by the Burdicks.

Moments after he did so he heard a sharp snapping report from somewhere not far off, and at practically the same instant felt a stinging sensation behind his right ear.

"Whoa, goddammit! There's somebody in here!" he called.

There was no response from outside, not even the sound of footsteps.

Peeved, Longarm felt behind his ear. His hand came away wet, and although it was too dark inside the outhouse for him to see, he knew good and well it was blood he was feeling.

Not much, though. A trickle, no more. He thought he could feel a small object that . . . "Dammit!" He jumped,

107

but there really was no need. The thing he'd touched pricked his inquiring finger and stung the nape of his neck besides. Probing again, more cautiously this time, he managed to extract a pine splinter about three fourths of an inch long and tapering to a very fine point that had been buried in Longarm's flesh just above the hairline.

He struck a match to examine the thing, and then used the light to inspect the side of the outhouse where the bullet—it pretty much had to have been a bullet—had come through the flimsy wall.

As nearly always, the inside surface was ripped wide open by the slug. The bullet had gouged a chunk out of the pine about half an inch wide and three or more inches long. But when he leaned close to thoroughly inspect the damage, Longarm could see that the entry hole on the other side of the damaged board was tiny. Perhaps as small as a .22 would have made, although in the soft pine it was impossible to judge that for sure.

Longarm lighted the candle that was fixed to the front wall of the outhouse and quickly finished wiping, then pulled his pants up and carried the candle outside with him to get a better look at the bullet hole.

The wood of the outhouse was old and dry and easily shattered, so it was impossible for him to be sure of the size of the slug that had come inside. But he still thought it could have been something as inoffensive as a little .22. Not exactly an ideal weapon of choice for anyone with serious intent, so the incident was no doubt an accident. And someone, no doubt, had been startled as hell by Longarm's shout when the splinter got his attention.

Still, both shooter and potential innocent victim had been damned lucky. The bullet had come in the side wall of the outhouse and passed directly above the pair of seats. If Longarm had been sitting upright instead of leaning forward to reach for the paper he could have been seriously hurt. And the fact that the shooting was accidental would not have made Longarm's pain any less.

Fortunately, the outcome proved no worse than mild annoyance. Longarm returned the candle to its shelf inside the outhouse and blew it out, then went to wash up. While he was at it he washed the blood off his neck and pressed a fingertip over the slightly stinging wound where the splinter had struck, making sure the tiny opening clotted over and the bleeding stopped. Then he went back inside and slipped out of the rubber boots.

As far as he could tell all the other passengers and stage line employees were at supper, although there was considerable movement to and from the buffet serving table and a sort of fluid shifting about of people, so it would have taken a deliberate focus of attention to determine if everyone was in fact present.

Not wanting to embarrass anyone, Longarm waited until Howard Burdick headed for the kitchen on some errand, then followed the station manager.

"Yes, Marshal? Something I can do for you?"

"I was wondering, Howard, if you have kids."

"What an odd question. But in fact yes, Jean and I have two daughters and a son."

"Mind at all. Our daughters are twenty and eighteen. Both are married. Ellie and her young man live in Illinois. He's a printer by trade. And our younger girl Elaine is up in Virginia City. They've opened a store there."

It wasn't the girls Longarm was interested in, but he saw no reason to interrupt Burdick because of that.

"Both girls married very fine young men, we are glad to say. As for our son, Glendon is in Bitter Creek. He boards there so he can attend the high school there. We want him to complete high school at the very least. College too if he is willing to take it on. Jean and I have hopes of him becoming a doctor or a lawyer or something fine like that." Burdick smiled. "Glendon himself has visions more on the order of being a cowboy. But then he is only fourteen. We're sure his views will change as he gets older."

Longarm frowned.

"Is there something wrong with that, Marshal?" Burdick asked.

"Pardon? Oh, uh, no, o' course not. An' I'm sure you're right. Boys grow up, thank goodness. I, uh, your son bein' in Bitter Creek isn't what I expected t' hear, that's all." He explained about the accidental shooting outside.

"What I figured," Longarm said, "was that you folks had a son, all right, but that he was out there tryin' to plink off some rats an' wasn't paying mind to where his bullets were going. But if the boy is down in town . . ."

"That really is odd, I grant you," Burdick agreed. "Quite apart from Glendon not being here, we don't have a rat problem. We used to until we got cats. Brought in two kittens, actually. That was several years ago. Now there are dozens of half-wild tabbies that live mostly in the hay-ricks and keep the rodents under control. And the owls and hawks and wild bobcats, of course, keep the cat population from getting out of hand. But . . . no, Marshal, there is no one around here who would have been shooting. Not at this hour when there is no light for target practice. For that matter, I don't own a .22. When we did used to shoot rats, it was always with a small-bore shotgun and light loads. I've never owned a rifle of any sort and never a pistol smaller than a .44."

"Damned strange, ain't it?" Longarm asked.

"Yes, it most certainly is."

"I, uh, don't s'pose you noticed anyone leave the place after I did."

"Marshal, I'm sorry. But the truth is that I never noticed *you* leave, much less anyone going out after you. Or before. It just wasn't . . ."

"Yeah. O' course. Sorry. Look, I'm sure it was an accident. Could o' been anything, someone walking out for a smoke or just t' be alone for a few minutes. Coulda thought he saw one of those bobcats or coulda mistook one o' your cats for a rat. For that matter coulda thrown a shot at a cat deliberately, just for the meanness of it. Likely we won't never know. An' it isn't important. There was no harm done, so we won't say nor do anything more about it, all right?''

''That is certainly fine with me if it is with you, Marshal. After all, you are the offended party.''

''Like I said, no harm done. We'll leave 'er be.''

''Good enough.'' Burdick motioned for Longarm to turn to his left. ''Lean down a minute and let me look at that. Jean has some salve if . . . no, I don't think you need medication. I can barely see where it hit you. Lucky it was just a splinter in that spot, though. If it had been the bullet, I suspect you would be a dead man now.''

''Yeah. Lucky,'' Longarm agreed. ''An' now I reckon I'd best go see what your good wife put on the table.'' He grinned ''Can't let those other rannies get too far ahead o' me, you know. Besides, I got to keep my strength up. The way things are going it could be quickest t' walk the rest of the way down t' Bitter Creek instead o' waiting for this mud to dry or freeze over.''

''I recommend the ham pot pie, Marshal. Jean outdid herself with that today.''

''Thanks for the tip, Howard. An' for the doctoring.''

''Any time, Marshal.'' Burdick paused and frowned. ''Not that I mean you should need more doctoring. I just meant . . .''

Longarm chuckled. ''I know what you meant, Howard. An' I thank you. Now if you'll excuse me, I've developed a fine hunger all of a sudden, an' it's gonna take some ham pot pie t' satisfy my needs.''

Burdick, he discovered, was right. The pot pie was exceptional.

As for the accidental shooting, he let the matter drop without looking to embarrass anyone.

# Chapter 25

The day had been such a bitch for everyone concerned that there was no thought of the visitors sitting up late talking or reading or playing cards. The unspoken consensus seemed to be that the best thing was for everyone to go to bed early and hope tomorrow would be an improvement upon today.

Burdick's was set up as a relay station and eating establishment, but no one had made any real provision for the housing of guests. Rather the visitors were expected to eat while the mule team was being changed and then get back on the road. They were expected to be passers-through, not overnighters.

Consequently there were neither beds nor bedding to accommodate all the guests, and Howard and Jean Burdick had to scramble to try and make everyone more or less comfortable.

They resolved the issue by giving the station building over to the women, the two southbound whores and the one lady who was traveling north. Along, of course, with the Burdicks themselves in their own private quarters.

The menfolk were told they could bed down in the hay sheds adjacent to the low-roofed barn and corral complex where all the mules were housed. The Burdicks had a few spare blankets over and above those deemed necessary for the comfort of the women. These they laid out for the men to use, although there were only four blankets and, including the stagecoach crews, fifteen men to share them.

Longarm liked these other fellows well enough, he supposed. But he damn sure didn't like them *that* well that he intended crawling under a blanket with one or more of them, not even the cleanest of them. The hell with that.

And it wasn't like there was any biting cold to have to overcome anyhow.

Hell, if it were cold enough that a man couldn't sleep in a hay pile, it would have been cold enough for the ground to freeze and they wouldn't have had this problem to begin with.

Longarm wished it would up and get bitter, nasty, miserable cold.

Then they could hitch up the coach and make it on down the road to Bitter Creek, where the steel rails would make chinook winds and a whole damned sea of mud irrelevant.

As it was, well, he would settle for a hayrick to crawl into. He'd slept under worse conditions than that before, and almost certainly would have to again.

Howard Burdick handed out a couple of jugs of Indian whiskey for the men to share for nightcap purposes.

"No need to be shy about the stuff," Burdick told them. "I mixed it up myself, and all the ingredients are fit for the human stomach. No t'baccy juice or gunpowder in this, just good stuff." He grinned. "Oh, and maybe some floor sweepings too. But only *tasty* floor sweepings, I assure you." Most of the fellows responded with chuckles.

Tyler Overton reached into his pocket for a coin, but Burdick waved the offer away.

"No charge for this whiskey, gents. The line regrets your inconvenience and will stand treat for whatever you eat and drink while you're here. Get a good rest, all of you, and hopefully tomorrow will be a better day."

113

Longarm, and he was sure everyone else too, could damn sure second that sentiment.

He accepted a pull at the jug when one came around to him. The raw grain alcohol base was solid, and whatever Howard had added to it—plenty of water and some caramel coloring, no doubt, plus whatever other odds and ends might have been handy—resulted in a mixture that was palatable if not exactly outstanding. As Indian whiskeys went it was better than many, perhaps even most. It wasn't going to give any competition to any bonded rye Longarm had ever tasted, not even the poorer grades of rye whiskey. But hell, the price was right and the attitude generous. Longarm wasn't going to bitch about it. He took a healthy slug and then another, the heat of the liquor spreading pleasantly through his belly, and then passed the jug along to the fellow beside him, the undersized dandy with the fancy cane.

"Than'kew," the little fellow said as if it were one word.

"You're welcome."

Longarm's temporary neighbor took a wee sip of the harsh whiskey—obviously doing his best to fit into a circumstance that was not what he was really accustomed to—and handed the jug on to someone else.

"If you'd follow me now, gents," Burdick said. "We only have a few lanterns, so I'll lead you out and leave you there for the night. Careful where you walk now. And those of you without rubber boots, you can decide for yourselves if you want to go barefoot in the mud and try to clean up a little when you get to the barn or wear your shoes and get them fouled all over again. Those of you with boots will please take them off once we reach the barn. You can leave all the boots by the door if you please. That way they can be used by anyone who needs to step outside during the night, either to go to the outhouse or to smoke. Which I must ask you to do outside, if you please, gents. Not that the mules give a damn, but the company would be very unhappy if that hay were to catch fire. For that matter, not all of you would likely appreciate it either. So for the safety of all I will ask the smokers among you to step outside. Any questions?''

There were none, and after a moment Burdick nodded and picked up his lantern. ''In that case, gentlemen, please be so good as to follow me.''

The actual barn was in the center of what amounted to a livestock complex. Corrals extended out behind the centrally located barn, and on either side of that center structure were wing-like extensions where hay was stored—a fine grade of bright timothy, Longarm noted, and not merely locally mowed wild hay—as well as rat-proof barrels of grain.

The grain barrels were ranked along the front walls of the forage shelters, while the expensive high-quality hay had been tightly packed inside the protection of the roofs. At this time of year hay had been drawn from both sides of the storage areas, leaving open floor space where beds could be made.

''Feel free to pull hay down and use it to sleep on. Or under if you like. We'll fork it back in place when you leave. Just remember not to smoke in here and if you need to take a piss, please go outside to do that. Don't piss in the hay, gentlemen, because if it doesn't come a freeze by tomorrow night you could be sleeping in here again. Or for several days to come. If you, um, see what I mean.''

A caution like that should have been unnecessary, but unfortunately, as Longarm knew from long experience, there were men whose laziness would lead them to do the damnedest things. Including pissing out of second-story windows rather than bothering to go downstairs to take their leak. If left to their own devices, it was entirely possible that one or more of the men right here in this bunch might choose to piss on his neighbor's bedding rather than go to the trouble of pulling cold rubber boots on and going out into the night.

"Good night, gentlemen. If you need anything"—Burdick paused for a moment and grinned,—"ask me about it in the morning."

Again the stage line passengers and crewmen rewarded their host with a chuckle as Howard Burdick took the lantern—Longarm suspected Burdick was more concerned with the likelihood of fire than he was about needing that lantern inside the station building—and went back to join the womenfolk in the stove-heated comfort of the main building.

The male passengers stumbled and grunted their way around, dividing without plan or pattern to make beds for themselves in the two separate hay storage areas.

And, inevitably, lighting their way with bright-flaring matches while they did so, never mind Howard Burdick's fears about the possibility of fire.

They were one damned weary bunch, though, and it was not long at all until all that could be heard inside the barn was the sound of loud snoring and the occasional stamp of a mule's hoof.

Longarm himself was at least as tired as anyone else, and made no attempt to stay awake and listen to the symphony his fellow passengers were putting on with their night music.

# Chapter 26

Longarm thought his bladder was gonna bust. They said if a man couldn't sleep the night through without taking a piss it was a sure sign of old age. Well then, count him old and crotchety because he damn sure had to go. Bad. Of course it might have as much to do with all the coffee he'd had with supper as it did with age.

Whatever the reason, though, it was a nuisance. He was comfortable as a beetle in a cow pie, and really did not want to stir out of the cocoon of sweet timothy he'd fashioned for himself next to the line of grain barrels at the front of the hay shed.

He was almost tempted to ignore Howard Burdick's good advice and just let fly. Like behind the barrels. Except wouldn't that be a disgusting thing to do. Pity, though. He really did not want to be bothered getting up and going outside.

On the other hand, the darkest cloud can have a silver lining. And in addition to taking a leak he had a real yen for a smoke. Howard Burdick didn't carry any of the excellent cheroots that Longarm favored, and all Longarm's spares were up the road a piece, in his bag still on top of the mud-stranded Concord. But Burdick did have a box of fairly decent cigars that he sold to travelers, and Longarm had put some of those in his pocket after dinner. So if he had to get up and leave the comfort of this hay nest, he might as well get some pleasure out of it.

He felt around in the dark for his vest and coat and pulled them on before he rose. Not just out of habit either. It might not be cold enough to turn the sloppy mud into ice, but it was plenty cold enough be a bother to a man in shirtsleeves if he was dumb enough to stand around outdoors.

Longarm buckled his gunbelt on too—pure habit that was coupled with a reluctance to leave his gun out of his own sight but within the reach of strangers, never mind that all those strangers were peacefully asleep and no threat to him anyhow—and made his way silently to the open doorway.

A hint of starlight, not so much light as it was a slight lessening of the darkness, let him find the row of gum boots left there. He stepped into a pair, the rubber cold and clammy on his bare feet, and went outside.

The night air was fresh and clean in his lungs after the sharp, ammoniac atmosphere inside the barn. He walked around to the side of the barn to piss, not bothering to go all the way around to the shitters, then leaned against the barn wall and pulled out one of the pale, slim panetelas he'd gotten from Howard.

He bit off the small twist at the pointed end of the cigar and mouthed the wrapper leaf for a moment. There was no hint of sweetness to the tobacco. A definite good sign of quality. Cigar makers try to mask poor grades of tobacco leaf by adding syrups, molasses, honey, rum, brandy, or whatever else they can think of that might disguise the harshness of the smoke produced by burning a lousy leaf.

This tobacco might not be the very best-quality leaf, but at least it was good enough that the maker was letting it stand on its own.

Longarm fired up his cigar and drew the smoke deep into his lungs, enjoying the flavor thoroughly.

He was still standing there savoring the night and the

smoke and the sprinkling of stars that were bright overhead when inside the barn he heard a sharp crackle of unexpected sound.

The sound was, he thought, suspiciously like that of a .22 pistol being fired.

He hoped no one had been hurt in there.

# Chapter 27

The dark hay shed was alive with sleepy, querulous conversation when Longarm got in there. Everyone seemed to be trying to speak at once, and most of the voices were all demanding to know the same thing: What happened and who did it?

"Does somebody have a match?" one voice called, overpowering the rest. "I got a candle some-damn-place here but I can't find my matches."

Longarm thumbed a lucifer aflame and held it up so he could find the man with the candle. It turned out to be one of the pair of northbound passengers who looked like mining engineers or surveyors, both of them pretty much peas from the same pod with rough but expensive clothing, knee-high lace-up boots, and narrow-brimmed fur felt hats of the very highest quality. Longarm took the few steps to his side and touched his match to the wick of the candle stub the man was holding.

Once they had some light to see each other by, the buzz of disjointed conversations slowed and withered away into a bleary-eyed and glowering silence.

"Does anybody know what happened?" Longarm asked.

"Not me."

"Huh-uh."

"I was sound asleep."

There were five men in addition to Longarm, and each disclaimed any knowledge of what had caused the commotion, although everyone had certainly heard it plainly enough. All had been jolted awake by the abrupt little explosion.

Each man certainly appeared to be telling the truth, Longarm thought.

In addition to himself—and because of the darkness he actually hadn't known beforehand just who his sleeping companions were—this side of the hay storage was accommodating Tyler Overton, the two engineers, the diminutive northbound gent with the cane, and the salesman Delmer Jelk.

"It sounded like a gunshot. That's what I think," Jelk offered.

"It was a gun. Had to be."

"All right, so who fired the shot? And at what?" Longarm asked.

No one answered.

"Tyler?"

"Wasn't me, Long."

"You, mister?" he asked the man who was holding the candle.

"Not me."

"You?"

The fellow shook his head.

"Delmer?"

"Nope."

"You, sir?"

"Certainly not."

Longarm shrugged. "Look, could anybody have sort of, I dunno, rolled over an' touched off a shot? You know, kinda accidental like?"

Again there was a round of denials, although Jelk went to the trouble of pulling a stubby bulldog revolver out of his coat pocket and sniffing the barrel to make sure the gun had not somehow discharged by accident while he slept.

"All right, if it wasn't a gun goin' off, what else could it have been?" Longarm inquired.

"It was a gun. Not a big one but a gun for sure," the candle-holder's companion asserted. "I've heard more than enough guns to know. This here was a gun going off."

"Fine," Longarm said. "You're bedded down kinda in the middle of things. Which side o' you was the gun fired on. Left? Right? Can you remember?"

The man frowned, lay down on the soft hay, and turned his face first in one direction, then in the other. After a few moments he shook his head. "I been trying to bring it back to mind. You know? But I was sleeping hard. I'm damned if I could say which way the sound came from. I mean, if it'd happened a second time, after I started to come awake, I'm sure I could tell you. But as it is . . ." He spread his hands wide, palms upward, and shrugged.

"Can anyone else recall?"

No one could.

"How about somebody not in this room? Could somebody else have come in from the other side, or someplace else for that matter, and fired one off? Into the roof for a prank or like that?"

"If it was a prank, Marshal, it was a piss-poor one."

"But could it have been that?"

"Marshal, it coulda been any damn thing except sensible. And it wasn't me that done it. That's all I'm sure of," Delmer Jelk claimed.

"That about covers it as far as I can see," Overton agreed. "We were all asleep, you know. None of us could testify to anything of a factual nature. At best we can only speculate."

Longarm frowned. He hated coming up against anything that he did not understand.

Still, no harm seemed to have been done.

"The hell with it," he said, taking advantage of the candlelight to return to his nest of warm, soft hay and pull a

122

mound of the sweet-smelling timothy over him. "G'night, gents," he said, and rolled over to resume his sleep.

A couple of the men, now that they were awake anyway, took the opportunity to go outside, presumably to relieve their bladders, and the others lay down again. Once everyone was back in their beds, the engineer extinguished his candle and the shed was once more plunged into darkness.

Longarm waited until he was again surrounded by snoring and then, without any particular anxiety but just as a matter of common-sense precaution, shifted the location of his bed by a good five or six feet.

Just in case.

After all, that was twice this evening that he'd been damn-all near to a small-caliber gunshot, and one of those had passed within inches of him. Who was to say if the second hadn't also come his way, or toward the place where he had been sleeping minutes beforehand.

He could see no reason for taking chances regardless of how slight the possibility of danger was.

Caution, after all, only hurts when you ignore it.

# Chapter 28

Longarm was sitting upright, .44 Colt already in hand, before he had time to consciously register what it was that had snapped him so rudely out of his sleep.

A gunshot. Another damn gunshot. And again of very small caliber, again sounding like the sharp, bitter little bark of a .22 pistol.

And at very close range.

Ignoring the hay that filtered maddeningly into his shirt collar, and ignoring as well the sudden hubbub of noise as the other men in the shed sat up in angry consternation, Longarm tried to recall the minuscule details of the sound that had so jarred him.

Sharp and biting, that was obvious on the surface of it. But . . . left. It had come from his left. He frowned, realizing that of course it had come from his left. He was sleeping at the front of the shed, dammit. Everything else was to his left as he lay with his head toward the end wall and his feet to the passage into the central part of the stage line's mule barn.

No, he thought. The fact that the noise had come from his left was useful after all. It meant the gun was fired by someone among his sleeping companions in this side of the barn. Someone coming in from the other hay shed, say, or from outside somewhere would have fired from the passageway. And that sound would have come from below Longarm's feet when he lay sleeping. So it was instructive after all to remember that the sound was to his left.

Apart from that . . . apart from that he couldn't remember shit. Dammit.

"Who's got a match?" the engineer's voice called out.

Longarm was a good dozen feet away, but someone else responded. The other engineer, it proved to be. The man struck a match and applied the flame to his friend's candle, bathing the hay shed in dim yellow light.

As far as Longarm could tell, every bastard in the place was lying—or by now for the most part sitting—in exactly the same places they'd been after the previous excitement.

Everyone, that is, except for himself. He had moved half a dozen feet or so toward the end wall after the others went to sleep. He couldn't help but wonder now . . .

While the others were asking themselves the same questions over and over again—and coming up with the predictable if uninformed responses—Longarm shoved his Colt into his waistband and knee-walked through the soft hay to the place where he'd been bedded before and where his coat and Stetson still lay.

"Do me a favor, friend, an' hold that light so's I can see here, willya?"

The engineer did as he was asked, and Longarm grunted. Not with satisfaction, exactly, but at least now the noises were commencing to make some sense.

He was no believer in the likelihood of coincidence, and *three* small-caliber reports in the vicinity of one person seemed just a wee bit much to swallow.

And there was the proof of the pudding. There was a set of small holes marring the sides and back of his coat. The coat that, thankfully enough, had been lying folded on the hay and not wrapped tight around him while he slept.

The point, however, was that *some son of a mangy bitch tried to shoot him dead.*

125

And tried it, it now would seem, three damn times before the intended victim so much as caught on to the notion that some asshole was shooting at him.

Longarm was feeling a mite peeved over that. The bastard had gone and made three good tries before Longarm even knew he was being shot at.

You could make a case for the sonuvabitch being awfully damn good. Or simply plenty lucky.

Longarm, on the other hand, couldn't much bring himself to admire the unknown fellow's efforts.

And that, of course, was the most important question of all now that Longarm had satisfied himself that he knew why these noises kept happening.

Oh, finding out the why of it would be nice to learn too.

But mostly, yes, mostly by damn, he wanted to find out *who*!

Well, the list of possibilities was short.

Tyler Overton, Delmer Jelk, the two engineers, and the dandy.

Longarm looked at each of them.

Far as he could read the deal, there was only one who knew him well enough to work up a reason to want him dead.

After all, Jelk seemed a simple enough traveling salesman with no possible motive. And the three northbound passengers not only could not have known they would run into a federal lawman, once they did—even if they had reason to hate and fear federal lawmen in general or Custis Long in particular—the only thing any of them would have had to do to get away from him was to sit down, shut up, and wait. As soon as the mud either dried or froze, Longarm would be on his way south and they would be headed just as quickly to the north.

Tyler Overton on the other hand . . .

Shit, Longarm didn't know of any motive the lawyer might have to stop him from possibly helping Gary Lee **Bell escape the hangman's noose.**

126

But he could think of a fair number of possibilities if he wanted to. Maybe none of them true. But who the hell could say?

For instance, Gary and Madelyn Bell were convinced her father's mine at Talking Water was pretty well worthless. But what if their lawyer knew something about the mine that they didn't? And wanted Bell dead and Maddy up to her pretty ears in debt to ensure that the mine would become Overton's property by and by.

Or to run out another possible motive, maybe Overton and the pregnant soon-to-be widow were putting on a big act about wanting Gary Lee Bell saved but really wanted him dead, by the law's cold hand and not theirs, so Overton could dump his mousy wife and take up permanent residence in Maddy's overheated bed.

Or it could be that the tipster from the Medicine Bows was right and Windy Williams was down there alive and well and full of piss. It could be that Overton was being paid something under the counter by Williams so the old curmudgeon—which he damn sure was—could rid his daughter of a husband Windy did not approve of.

Or . . . or, hell, there could be a hundred other "or" possibilities.

And maybe not a one of them that Longarm could think of was true, but then maybe there was some other explanation, crazy to everyone else but perfectly logical and inescapable in the mind of Attorney Tyler Overton, that was in hiding needing only to be identified.

Longarm sighed. He could fret about the "why" of it all at leisure some other time.

Right now he was mostly interested in seeing to the "who" of it—which he sure as shit figured he had—and making damn sure there was no fourth, and perhaps successful, attempt on his life.

Damn it anyway, though . . .

"Tyler?"

"Yes, Long?"

127

"I'd be obliged if you would hold your hands kinda out t' the side where I can keep an eye on 'em. An' you, mister. Hold that candle nice an' steady. It wouldn't much do for anybody t' get confused and excited just now."

"What the . . . ?"

Longarm ignored the engineer, his attention closely focused on Overton instead.

The lawyer, he had to admit, acted innocent as a duck in the henhouse. Which didn't mean a damn thing.

"Keep 'em right where I can see them, Tyler, while I shake your tree an' see what kind of shooting irons fall out."

# Chapter 29

"Well, I'll be a son of a bitch," Longarm complained.

"I think I am beginning to agree with you," the engineer with the candle—the one who used to have a candle, that is, for the stub had long since burned away and the search had continued by the growing daylight—put in. "Are you going to finish soon so we can go have breakfast?"

"You'll go when I say you can go, goddammit," Longarm snapped.

But then his sleep had been twice interrupted too. And for a much more personal reason than any of these others.

The engineer saw the tight-kept fury lingering at the back of Longarm's glare and shut his mouth.

The problem was that after stripping Tyler Overton buckass naked and searching every stitch of thread the man had been wearing, Longarm had not been able to locate so much as a sniff of the pistol that had been fired at him.

After searching Overton himself Longarm had searched through the hay in the vicinity of Overton's makeshift bed.

At that point Longarm had figured he could fully appreciate the implications of the old saying about looking for needles in haystacks.

Which had not, of course, kept him from continuing the search.

He'd inspected first the man, then the bedding, and finally all the loose hay, the nooks and crannies, every possible place where a pistol could be tossed in the darkness by a man lying where Tyler Overton had chosen to make his bed.

He had not found shit.

Yet.

"All right, dammit, someone has it. Let's see about the rest of you. Delmer? Strip."

"What?"

"You heard me. I want your clothes."

"But . . ."

"Look, either I inspect your clothes after you hand 'em to me or I do it while you're wearing 'em. An' if you make me go over there an' play with your balls, Delmer, I'm gonna be even more pissed off than I already am. I might not be real gentle about it. You see what I mean?"

"Uh, yeah, I think I do." Jelk began hastily pulling off his shirt and trousers.

After a few moments the others did too.

In light of Longarm's cold anger the others did not object. Not even the dandy.

As before, though, there was no sign of any small-caliber handgun.

Jelk had his English .455 bulldog. One of the engineers was carrying a pocket-model Colt, one of the short-barreled guard models with no sights and no ram for shell ejection, but a full .45 caliber in spite of its small size. And the little fellow with the cane had a positively wicked folding penknife with gold handles and a rusting blade.

Those were the only weapons Longarm could find in the crowd.

*There was no damned gun!*

Except . . . except someone had fired at him. With a gun. Three damn times.

There had to be an explanation. Of course there was. There was always an explanation. The only trick was finding out what the hell that explanation might be.

And in this case Longarm was beginning to think that the explanation, however logical and simple it might really be, was somewhere way over his head.

Maybe he was more tired than he realized. Not thinking straight. Or something.

"Aren't you guys done in there yet?" George, the coach jehu, called from the doorway for probably the twelfth time. "Miz Burdick is getting upset about breakfast going so cold and her with still so many to feed."

Longarm sighed. "Tell her we're on our way, George."

Hell, they might as well go eat. He wasn't accomplishing anything in here.

"We can go now?" one of the engineers said.

"Yeah," Longarm said in a low, defeated voice. "Everybody can go now."

The men finished buttoning and tucking and made their way swiftly out of the hay shed and on to the station building, where their meal had long since been waiting. The men who'd slept in the other hay shed were probably finished eating by now and the food was no doubt as cold as a new-caught trout.

The only one of the other men who did not make a rush for the table, oddly, was Tyler Overton. He hung back.

"Yes? What d'you want?" Longarm demanded.

"I just wanted . . . I wanted to tell you that I harbor no grudge here. I understand."

"You do?"

"You haven't exactly been forthcoming about why you did all that, Long, but it doesn't take any genius to work it out. Someone shot at you. And since I am the only one who really knows you, and knows why you are here and the mission you are embarked on, it's only natural that I would be your prime suspect. Well, I just wanted to say that I understand. I'm sure I would come to the same conclusions if our situations were reversed. I don't blame you and I don't resent the search. And I . . . I'm not sure how

131

you will take this, Long, but I mean it sincerely. If I can help in any way . . ."

Longarm gave the Talking Water lawyer a long, searching look. Then he scowled, as much in confusion as for any other reason. "Yeah. Thanks, Tyler." He managed a weak smile. "I think."

Overton nodded. "Like I say, Long. The offer is sincere. Any time. Any way I reasonably can."

Longarm chuckled. "Now there's a lawyer for you, all right. Even an offer like that you're careful t' qualify. Anything you 'reasonably can,' huh?"

Overton laughed. "Really, Long. You can't expect me to ignore years of careful training surely."

"No. But if you weren't the one shooting at me . . ."

"Then who could it have been? And why? Am I right?"

"Afraid so, Tyler. I reckon I'm 'feared that you are."

"May I make a suggestion?"

"Yeah, shoot." Longarm grinned. "Figuratively speakin', that is."

"Let's ponder those questions *after* breakfast, shall we? I for one am damned well hungry." He patted his more than ample belly as a reminder that he was a trencherman of no small consequence.

"Yeah," Longarm reluctantly agreed. "Reckon we ought to."

Innate caution, though, made him hold back so Overton could take the lead on the way to the station building. Longarm had just established beyond any shred of doubt that the lawyer was unarmed. Even so . . .

# Chapter 30

By the time Longarm and the lawyer joined the others inside the station building, everybody in the place knew about the gunshots that had, presumably, been directed at the deputy U.S. marshal during the night.

That was not the way Longarm would have preferred it. There are times—in fact, most of the time—when it is better to listen than to talk, he figured. And generally speaking, he would prefer to be the one to make any announcements or declarations concerning . . . well, concerning just about anything affecting him personally or the conduct of his job. He tried to be pleasant and friendly enough with anyone who would allow it. But he wasn't much when it came to blabbing every thought that passed through his head.

It was damn sure too late for that here. As soon as he walked in he was greeted with sympathetic comments from some and by big-eyed looks from the rest of the folks who were stranded at Burdick's station.

Howard Burdick himself was apologetic as hell about the whole thing.

"Hell, Howard, it ain't your fault. And you didn't do nothing. I know that. It was somebody sleeping in that same room with me that did the shooting. That leaves you and your missus out of it. And these ladies here an' half the

133

rest o' the menfolk on hand.''

Telling that to Burdick was enough to remind himself of it. And remind him as well that the fact of the shootings being common knowledge among the others should have no ill effect. After all, the shooter—whoever the sonuva-bitch was—knew that Longarm was alerted now. The futile search for the pistol in the hay shed had made sure the shooter was warned.

So probably there was no harm done if the rest of the crowd knew about it too.

Still, Longarm was one who liked to keep his own counsel and not give out any information without a good and specific reason.

Longarm made a point of sitting beside Tyler Overton during breakfast. After all, if everyone knew about the shootings they would also know that Overton had been Longarm's first suspect as the assassin. Better to avoid forcing any labels onto the lawyer by making a show of friendship with him now.

What the onlookers wouldn't be able to tell, of course, was that Overton was *still* Longarm's primary suspect for being the nighttime shooter.

But a clever one.

Where in *hell* had he—or, okay, who-the-hell-ever—hidden that pistol?

It hadn't been on his person. Longarm would swear to that. Hadn't been on him or any of the other men who'd been in that hay shed.

And the damn thing almost certainly hadn't been hidden anywhere in there either.

Longarm had practically examined the hay stems one by one in that whole huge stack. And even though there hadn't been time enough for anyone to shoot, cross the room, and then get back to his bed before the others stirred and started striking matches, Longarm had gone so far as to pry up the lid of each and every grain barrel and feel around inside them too.

The gun wasn't anyplace.

That he could find.

Except, dammit, everything has to be *some*place.

If a gun existed—and a gun for sure did exist—then it naturally had to be somewhere. If only Longarm could find it.

"The boys have been telling us about the excitement over there last night and your search for the weapon. We'll go out after breakfast," Burdick offered, "and move all that hay out of the room. I can close off a couple stalls in the barn and move it in there. Take everything out to the bare walls and floor. Could be your man buried it or something like that. If we take all the hay out and sweep the floor, we'll be able to see if anyone dug a hole or found a crack in the wall boards or the like."

"That's mighty nice o' you, Howard. It's a lot o' work, I know."

"It's important," Burdick said. "The line will do it gladly. Any volunteers to help?" he added in a slightly louder voice.

"George and me," Jesse offered. "We'll pitch in." He looked around. "So will Roy and Charlie." This appeared to come as something of a surprise to the crew of the north-bound coach, but they did not seem inclined to argue the point with the take-charge driver of the other coach.

"Anyone else?" Burdick asked.

Leonard Grohle fidgeted a little but stopped short of speaking up. The cowhand looked away, an expression of mild embarrassment on his face and a hint of flush creeping into his earlobes. All the rest of the gents put on frozen expressions and acted like the suggestion couldn't possibly have anything to do with them.

Longarm was disappointed. When this subject came up he had hoped that the shooter would be quick to jump in with an offer to help, acting on the theory that he couldn't be thought guilty if he was so eager to assist.

135

It looked like the sonuvabitch was too smart to identify himself that easy. Dammit.

As it turned out, though, the only men willing to help with the work were coach line employees. And all of them had been sleeping elsewhere when the shootings occurred. If Longarm wanted a break here he was going to have to find it elsewhere.

"Is that it?" Burdick asked. "All right then, boys. We'll head over to the barn straightaway when we're finished with our coffee."

"Mighty kind o' you," Longarm told them. And meant it. Inwardly, of course, he was grumbling that the shooter hadn't tripped himself up.

But then a man can't have everything.

And under the circumstances, Longarm figured he should be pleased that he'd had an opportunity this morning just to wake up.

That right there was a good enough start to any day, he figured. Especially when there was someone around who wanted to make contrary arrangements.

"Two . . . no, make that three . . . more o' those fine flannelcakes," Longarm said, "an' I'll be right with you." He gave Jean Burdick a smile of appreciation and reached for the platter of light, fluffy cakes and the crockery jug of corn syrup to sluice over them.

# Chapter 31

"Marshal." The voice was a barely heard whisper.

"Huh? What?" He looked around. But could not figure out at first who it was who had spoken. The only person close by was the mystery woman in the blue gown and heavy veil. And she was looking away, not seeming to pay the least bit of attention to him.

"Not so loudly, please," the voice said.

He looked in both directions and concluded that, all right, it pretty much had to be the woman in blue who was doing the whispering. But what . . . ?

"Do not look at me, please. I must speak with you, Marshal. The information I have to give is vital, yes?"

"I, uh, yeah I reckon we can talk, ma'am."

"Please, Marshal. Softly. No one must overhear. No one must suspect I talk with you." There was, Longarm thought, a faint hint of accent in her voice. Something Slavic maybe. But he was not sure of that. Hell, he could barely hear her at all, much less figure her out from her speech.

"How d'you figure us t' talk if . . ."

"Outside. The people here, they expect you to follow Mister Burdick and the men. Out to the barn, they said. You leave now. But you do not go to the barn, no. You go out back. Into the rest house that is set aside for the ladies. In few minutes I will go out. Into the rest house. You wait for me there. When we are finished speaking I will leave first, make sure no one watches. Then I will tap on door and you will know it is safe to follow, yes?''

''Sounds all right t' me, I reckon,'' he whispered back while looking in another direction entirely.

The deception seemed silly as hell. But then he didn't know what the whole deal was here. The time to scoff would be *after* he had all the facts, not before.

Taking his time about it, Longarm fired up one of Howard Burdick's good panatelas and sat there for several moments letting the smoke wreathe his head while he savored the taste of the tobacco. Then he rose and left the table, stopping at the front door to slip into a pair of the cold and clammy rubber boots before going outside.

Across the muddy yard he could hear the sound of voices inside the barn where Burdick and the others were working to move the hay.

Longarm felt bad about letting them do all the work, but he didn't see that he had much choice. If the woman in blue knew something about the man who wanted to gun him, well, that was information he wanted pretty bad. He turned away from the barn and headed around back toward the outhouses.

He passed by the men's outhouse with the tiny hole in the side wall from where the first attempt had been made on Longarm's life. And him not so much as recognizing the shooting for what it was, dammit. He went on by, and hesitated when he got to the door of the ladies' outhouse.

It just purely wasn't in him to go waltzing in there without knocking. Shit, he'd be embarrassed half out of his mind if he walked in and found even one of the whores perched on the pot. And if he intruded on Mrs. Burdick? There weren't words enough in the English language to explain away a blunder like that. He tapped lightly on the

138

door and asked, "Anyone there? I say, is anyone in there, please?"

There was no response, and after another moment's hesitation he pulled the door open and stepped inside.

The shitter was empty. He was fascinated to discover, though, that it didn't smell at all like the men's two-holer. This one smelled almost . . . nice.

Then he saw the reason why. Beside the bin where the wiping paper was stored someone had put a little shelf. On it there was a bottle of patent toilet water—right well named in this instance, he thought—with a lantern wick jammed into the mouth of the bottle. The damp wick allowed the fragrance, lilac according to the label on the fancy little bottle, to escape slowly into the air, covering over much of the natural odor of such a facility and making the whole thing a much more pleasant place for a lady to drop her drawers.

Longarm sat down to wait—no need to fret here about an errant aim splattering piss on the toilet seat—and smoke his cigar.

"You will allow me?" the woman in the blue gown asked as, without waiting for a response, she reached up and plucked the cigar out of Longarm's mouth.

He let her take it without quarrel. Hell, he'd run into women more than once in the past who rebelled against the social restriction imposed upon the weaker sex and who in private might enjoy the taste of tobacco. Or other things generally forbidden to them.

He figured this woman was another one like that, and if she wanted a drag on his cigar, then . . . "Hey!"

His yelp came too late, and with horror he watched her drop the fine, pale panatela into the open maw of the dump hole. "What the hell did you do that for?"

"I am very sensitive to the smoke, no? You must not smoke in these close quarters. My lungs are delicate. But of course if you want your filthy thing back again, Marshal,

139

I will attempt to retrieve it for you.'' There was a sound from behind the veil that might have been muted laughter. "Of course you must first promise me that you will smoke the rest of it. Then I will be sure to recover it for you, no?''

"Thank you so much," he said in a dry tone.

"You do not want it now? So sad. It would have been amusing for us both, I think.''

"Not for us both," he said. "Look, inside the station you told me you know something 'bout this bird that wants to perforate my belly.''

"I did? I really said a thing like that?"

"That's what I took you t' mean.''

"But *non, mon cher,* that is not quite what I mean to say.''

"Then what . . . ?''

"I tell you I have information that is vital. But it is not about the man who would shoot you. Of that I know nothing. I would tell you if I knew. But I do not.''

"If not that, then . . . ?''

"The country. This country. It is in very great danger, Marshal. And you, as a representative of the government of this country, you are one to whom I can deliver my warning, yes?''

He gave her a questioning look. Information vital to the country? What the hell was this broad talking about?

"You wish to know what I have to say?''

"Well . . . yeah. Uh, yeah, I'm sure I do." If he happened to have reservations about that, well, he'd keep those to himself. For now.

"First you must do three things, Marshal," the woman said.

"Three?''

"Yah, three." First he'd thought the hint of accent was Slavic, and then maybe French, and now it sounded more like low German, or it could be Polish. Weird.

"So tell me—''

"Three things, Marshal. First you must promise absolute

140

secrecy. No one must know from whom you obtain this information. You do promise?''

"I reckon. I'll keep your name outa it so far as I can." He smiled. "Which oughta be pretty easy since I have no idea what your name is or what you look like."

If she smiled back at him he couldn't tell it because of the thick veil that shielded her features from view.

"The next thing, Marshal, is that your government must agree to pay me for this information. Twenty . . . no, we make it twenty-five t'ousand dollar. Is this agreed?''

"Ma'am, I don't know what it is you expect from me, but I'm just a deputy marshal. I got no authority to commit the government to payin' rewards or anything like that."

"But you will agree to tell your government what I ask? You will do that much?''

"I reckon I can promise that. I'll bring it up if I think your information warrants it. I just won't make you no promises that I can't be sure will be kept.''

"Yes, that is honest. I respect this. It is good enough, I think.''

"And the third thing?" Longarm asked.

"This is the third request, it is a matter of some delicacy. Very personal. This I do not want to talk about until everything is done.''

"I can't very well make you promises without knowin' what it is you want.''

"I will trust your integrity, Marshal.''

He shrugged. "If you're willin', ma'am, I reckon I am too. So, uh, what is it you want t' tell me?''

She leaned forward, glancing over her shoulder as if to see there was no one eavesdropping even though the two of them were standing belly to belly inside a one-hole with barely room enough to turn around. And then only if the other was careful to stand clear.

The woman in blue put her mouth close to Longarm's ear. He could feel the brush of rough mesh against his flesh and the heat of her breath coming through the veil.

She whispered hoarsely.

Longarm blanched a pale, shocked white.

Without thinking of what he was doing he balled his right hand into a fist and sent it wrist-deep into the veiled woman's gut.

As she doubled over in agony he shoved her down onto the toilet seat so as to get her the hell out of his way and bulled past her into the clean air outside.

The door hadn't more than had time to slap shut behind him when he heard the woman begin to laugh, the sound of it like a donkey's braying in the morning stillness.

"You're sick. You know that? Sick," he threw over his shoulder as he stormed out of the shitter.

He turned, intending to say more to the stupid cunt in blue, but was rudely interrupted by the sharp bark of a small-bore gunshot and the virtually simultaneous slap of a bullet striking the left side of his chest.

Longarm reeled back against the outhouse door.

# Chapter 32

Slumped against the door to a women's crapper was not his idea of a properly dignified place for a man to die. If, that is, any place could be so considered. But even so . . . He frowned. Dignified or not, if he was standing here dying why was it taking so long? And for that matter, why didn't it hurt where he'd been shot?

After all, he had been known to take lead before. And it sure hadn't felt like this ever before.

Was that because this wound was mortal and those others had been picayune in comparison?

That could be, he supposed, but shit, this time it didn't even hurt.

Oh, he'd felt it, all right. But the poke hadn't been very hard. Something on the order of a playful jab. Or the tap of a kid playing tag. But nothing serious.

Yet a gunshot in the chest, that was just about as serious as things got.

Wasn't it?

Longarm straightened, abandoning the support of the outhouse door he'd been leaning against, and stood upright. He slid a hand inside his coat and felt for the warm, sticky wetness of fresh blood. Or for the pain of an entry wound. Or . . . something.

All he found inside his coat was his shirt. No longer fresh, but dry and apparently unperforated.

He frowned a little more, this time in puzzlement, however, and not with any trace of disappointment. It came as something of a surprise to him—but definitely not a disagreeable one—to discover that the gunshot seemed to have done no damage.

He felt around a little more and then, comprehension commencing to dawn, pulled his wallet out.

There was a small hole in the front of his coat and a corresponding hole in the leather of his wallet. But no holes through the inside liner of the coat nor, most importantly, through Longarm himself.

When he opened the wallet it was to disclose his badge, the shape of the metal slightly altered from behind, a small bulge as it were. And when he unpinned the badge from the leather flap inside his wallet, a small, flattened lead projectile dropped into his palm.

Shee-it, he mumbled softly to himself. And then, aloud, he said, "Stay inside there, lady. Don't come out."

"Are you all right, Marshal? Did I hear—?"

"I said you're to stay inside an' I mean it. If you poke your head out I might go an' misunderstand what's happening an' put a .44 slug through the bridge o' your nose. You understand me?"

"Was that a shot that I heard, Marshal?"

"D'you understand me?" Longarm insisted.

"Yes, of course, but . . ."

He was no longer paying attention to the bitch in blue. She could wait.

Right now he had other things to think about.

He palmed his Colt and began a slow drift in the direction the gunshot had come from.

# Chapter 33

The back wall of Burdick's station was windowless. Plain and blank and with no defensive firing slits or other openings where a gun and gunman might be concealed. Which meant whoever had fired the shot that hit with deadly accuracy—albeit with fortuitous result for Deputy U.S. Marshal Custis Long—had to have been hiding at one corner or the other of the longish structure.

As close as Longarm could recall when he tried to bring the exact sound of the shot back to mind, the would-be assassin must have been on the south or right-hand side of the place.

Staying well clear of the building on the theory that the guy had had an aimed shot from rest at a stationary target, but that he couldn't be that accurate again if his quarry was at a distance and at the same time was in motion, Longarm skirted wide around the back of the place until he could get an unobstructed view of that side of the building.

As he pretty well expected, there was no one in sight.

Once again his small-bore attacker had made a swift, single attempt at murder and then . . . disappeared.

This was the fourth time the same man had taken a crack at him, Longarm reflected sourly, and he had not yet gotten so much as a glimpse of the sonuvabitch.

The man might was well have been a ghost. A will-o'-the-wisp.

What he most assuredly was *not* was imaginary.

Longarm had the misshapen lead slug in his pocket to prove that, the bit of distorted metal that had been stopped by the thickness of his leather wallet and the barrier of his badge of office.

Except for those—except for the accuracy of the gunman's aimed fire—Longarm could well be lying dead or dying at that very moment.

Whoever this bastard was, Longarm acknowledged, he was uncommonly good at his job.

And for him it was a job. Longarm would have willingly bet the farm on that assumption. Who except a paid professional, and a damned good one at that, would keep coming back for repeated tries after the first few failed. Most especially, who but a very confident professional would make this last attempt in broad daylight and from such a distance.

Longarm stopped for a moment to estimate the range from the back corner of the station building—which surely was the spot from which that shot had been fired—to the front door of the ladies' outhouse.

Forty yards? At least that, he decided.

A small-caliber pistol is a short-range firearm. Generally speaking, even in the hands of an expert, a .22 pistol could be considered to have an effective range of not more than fifteen yards. Twenty-five yards tops, and that was if the shooter had a solid rest for his hand.

Most handgun combat is undertaken, Longarm knew perfectly well, at distances of from two to eight yards. And never mind what the dime novels claimed. The people back East who wrote and printed them, Ned Buntline and his ilk, might not know any better, but Longarm and all his fellow peace officers damn sure did. Gunfights are mostly belly-to-belly affairs, and the man who is steady enough to draw a bead and take aimed fire from longer ranges is one mighty rare bird indeed.

This guy, though, had shot from an estimated . . . no, screw this estimated stuff. Longarm wanted to know for sure. He strode to the back corner of the station and, marching in a straight line, paced off the distance to the outhouse.

Forty-two yards. His guess had been close.

He looked back over his shoulder and reflected on the view of the outhouse he'd had from the ambusher's place of hiding. There was a square-on view of the door to the women's shitter, but the wider two-holer assigned to the men sat at a slight angle so that from that south end of the station building there was only an oblique view of the men's outhouse door. Anyone coming out of that outhouse would be momentarily screened from view by the swing of the wooden door itself, and if the victim then happened to move to his left instead of coming straight on, there would be no good shot at all. In order to be sure of getting a good shot at someone emerging from the men's outhouse an ambusher would have to set up at the north end of the station. And if he were standing there he would be in view of the men who were working in the barn.

Interesting, Longarm thought as he pondered the facts. Damned well interesting.

He pulled out a panatela—later on if the mud dried enough to be a little less sloppy, perhaps he could walk out to the stranded coach and get some of his own brand of cheroots; the panatelas were nice and he was grateful to have them, but they couldn't compare with his old favorites—and took his time about lighting the thing.

He puffed on the cigar for a few minutes while he rolled a few things around in his mind.

Then, satisfied, he said, "Reckon the excitement is over. You can come out now."

"I was afraid you'd forgotten me," the blue bitch's voice called from behind the closed outhouse door.

"No chance o' that," he assured her.

147

"Very well then." The door came open with a faint creaking of the rusty spring, and the veiled woman stepped outside to join Longarm.

"Turn around for a second, if you don't mind, please."

"Pardon me?"

"Please."

With a small shrug of her shoulders the woman turned to face away.

Longarm reached forward and quickly snapped the steel bracelet of a handcuff onto her left wrist, yanked it hard back, and clamped the other cuff securely on her right wrist.

"What the hell are you—?"

"It's best you should understand that I don't figure to screw around with you. You set me up, woman. You brought me out here deliberate as hell an' set me up t' be murdered in cold blood. Can't be no other way, as I see it. So don't expect no sympathy or gentle treatment. Long as you're in my custody, woman, you toe the line. Otherwise I put leg irons an' a gag on you too an' pack you in like a hog being carried to slaughter. And if you really give me trouble, it could happen that you'll be shot whilst trying t' escape. Understand?" The last was pure bullshit. But she didn't need to know that.

"I'll have your badge for this, damn you."

"You an' your boyfriend had your chance t' get that. Since you can't take it off my corpse, I reckon you got t' pay the penalty for failing. Now shut up an' hold still while I shake you down t' see if you're carrying iron."

Without further preamble he bent down and stuck a hand under the back of her gown. He intended to take no more chances with this murderous bitch and her as yet unknown playmate.

# Chapter 34

Shocked scarcely began to describe the expressions of the others stranded at Burdick's when Longarm brought the blue-gowned woman in wearing handcuffs—and, incidentally, cussing to make a mule skinner blush.

The woman sure as hell had a mouth on her.

In a few terse and well-chosen words Longarm explained just why it was he had put her under arrest. "Quick as I can get her before a federal judge," he concluded, "she'll be charged with conspiracy to assault a federal officer. Maybe some other stuff if I can get the U.S. attorney t' go along. Way I see it"—he paused to take a deep, satisfying drag on the cigar—"she'll do three years at the least, ten if we can finagle the deal so she comes up before old Judge Hardash. Hardass is what most call him behind his back. An' he owes me a favor besides."

"But why would this poor woman want to harm you, Marshal?" Jean Burdick asked.

"I'm not real sure 'bout that, ma'am. My guess is that her boyfriend got her t' do it. Hell, could be that's how she makes a living, setting men up for the boyfriend t' shoot."

Mrs. Burdick's hand flew to her throat in horror, and she looked wildly around at the men—all of them strangers to her—who were gathered in her common room.

If what Longarm claimed was true, one of these men was a deliberate, cold-blooded murderer. And likely had been for quite some time past.

"I think," Mrs. Burdick said, "we should get my husband in here. After all, he is in charge."

"Yes, ma'am. As you wish."

Longarm shoved the veiled woman onto a stool in a corner of the big room, being none too gentle about it, and growled, "Sit still if you like, or I can shackle you in place an' make sure of it. Your choice."

She said nothing. Because of the veil he could not see her expression. Likely that was a blessing, he decided.

"Long."

"Yes, Tyler?"

"Do you know who the woman's, um, alleged accomplice might be?"

Longarm's only answer was a wolfish grin.

Let the son of a bitch read that and work it out for himself, Longarm thought with grim satisfaction.

Mrs. Burdick was back within moments, Howard and all four other station employees trailing along behind her. Burdick looked concerned. The stagecoach crews looked like spectators gathering for a prizefight. Or perhaps something even more bloodily entertaining.

"What is this, Long? Have you really placed this lady under arrest?"

"Ayuh, I sure as hell have, Howard. Though I think it's kinda pushing credibility t' call her a lady."

Longarm took hold of the brim of her chapeau and gave it a yank, pulling away hat and veil alike.

The woman who was revealed to view had auburn hair and hard features, her cheeks marred by childhood pox scars and her mouth set in a thin, furious scowl. She had pale eyes and uncommonly thick eyebrows.

It took him several moments of searching through his memory to come up with a name to go with those features.

"I'll be damned."

"That's the first true thing you've said yet, you son of a bitch," the woman told him.

"Clementine Bonner, right?"

"Up yours, shithead."

"Yeah, that's you, all right." To the others in the big room he said, "Miss Bonner is on a gracious plenty of wanted posters. Mostly from Nebraska, Missouri, some from Illinois an' Minnesota, if I remember a'right. The lady's specialty, y'see, is murder. She'll spot a mark she thinks has a wad o' cash on him an' bat her eyelashes some. Though God knows why anybody'd want t' make the two-back beast . . . uh, excuse me, Miz Burdick, I kinda forgot m'self there."

"Your apology is accepted, Marshal. Please continue."

"Yes, ma'am." He touched the brim of his Stetson in Mrs. Burdick's direction, then went on. "Clementine here likes to get a fella drunk an' take him off somewhere private. Except while he's busy gettin' his pants off, she sidles up behind an' makes like she's gonna hug him. Least that's the way we figure it from what's found afterward. Nobody's ever survived t' tell us for sure. Thing is, she gets behind a fella like that an' slips a loop o' piano wire over his head. One good tug is all it takes. A garrote, I think the rig is called. It crushes the windpipe. Pull real hard an' it can practically cut a man's head off. Though I don't think she's ever quite managed t' accomplish that. Came close a few times, though." Longarm smiled. "There's some lawmen I know over east of here that're gonna be real happy t' see Clementine sitting in a federal prison where they can file extradition papers on her."

"You bastard," she hissed.

"You'd have t' ask my folks 'bout that, not me," Longarm responded.

"Trust me."

"Yeah, Clementine, I'll just do that. You bet."

"But what about the man who shot at you?" Burdick

151

asked. "You say she has been working with someone here?"

"That's right. Murder for hire would be my guess. Though who would want me dead I really don't know." He smiled, although no mirth reached his eyes. "Not anyone in particular, that is. For sure, though, I never seen any of these fellows before this trip here. An' none of them is on any posters that I know about. So whatever reason someone has for wanting me dead, I'd say it's a cash transaction an' our boy is a professional gunman."

"A gunfighter using a .22 pistol?" Burdick asked, his voice expressing rather obvious disbelief.

"That reminds me, Howard. You an' the other fellows can quit looking for that gun. I thank you for your effort, but there's no pistol hidden over there t' be found."

"But how—?"

"Right under my damn nose," Longarm said. "The whole time the gun was right under my nose an' I never noticed."

"I don't understand," Burdick said.

"None of us did. Which was the whole point o' this guy's way o' doing business. You know how Clementine has her favorite weapon an' method? Well, so does her boyfriend. An' I got to say that he's a kinda clever sonuvabitch. Until you figure it out, that is."

Longarm dipped two fingers into his vest pocket and pulled out the scrap of misshapen lead that had caught inside his wallet a little while earlier.

"This right here is what gave him away," he said with a great deal of satisfaction.

At the rear of the crowd that had gathered close around Longarm and his prisoner there was a slight stir.

People began edging nervously away in anticipation of more gunplay.

# Chapter 35

"Oh, I don't think you folks got much t' worry about here. My guess is that our boy would rather take his chances in a court o' law than standing face to face against me with a six-gun." Longarm grinned.

"Isn't that so, little fella?" he asked the mild, meek-looking little dandy with the cane and the fancy clothes.

"Me? You would accuse me? But really, sir. You searched me yourself this morning. All these gentlemen saw. I had no revolver then and I have none now."

"That's right, mister. You didn't have no revolver. Nor no pistol o' any kind. That's just as true as true can be."

"Then surely, sir, you cannot think—"

"Oh, but I do. An' I can prove it easy enough. You think you still got the wool pulled down over my eyes? 'Fraid not, mister . . . what is your name anyhow?"

The little man straightened to his full height. Which was at least half a head shorter than Longarm even so. "I, sir, am Herbert Amos Hancock."

"Called?"

"*Mister* Hancock to you, sir," the little man said with a brave show of haughty disdain.

"Yeah, sure, Herbie," Longarm drawled. "You wanta lay down your gun now, please?"

"I already told you, Marshal. I have no firearm. As you yourself determined not two hours ago."

"Herbie, lemme put it this way. I can show these folks what I mean after I take the thing off your dead body. Which I will damn sure do—shoot you down, that is—if you don't lay down the weapon. I can take it that way or else you can hand it over nice an' quiet, after which time you an' me will talk about a deal."

"A deal, sir?"

"Ayuh. The big thing you win is that you get to keep on breathing for a spell. Second thing is that once we chat, an' you tell me who it is that hired you . . . and why . . . then I tell the judge how cooperative you been and—"

"Marshal. Marshal Long? Listen to me." It was Clementine Bonner. Longarm wasn't real surprised. If there were favors going to be passed around, Clementine would want to make sure she was first in line and to hell with her erstwhile partner.

"Yes, Clemmie?"

"Now wait just a minute there, Marshal," Herbert Amos Hancock rushed to say. "It was me you offered the deal to, not that woman."

Longarm was not exactly amazed. There is damned small sign of loyalty among criminals. They might talk about "honor among thieves," but the truth of the matter is more "devil take the hindmost" than any sort of honor or decency. But then, hell, why would you expect decency out of criminals anyhow?

"Y'know, Herbie, you're running it right close t' the line seeing as how you still haven't laid down that gun of yours."

Hancock dropped his cane like the duck-head grip had of a sudden become burning hot.

"What the hell?" someone in the room asked of no one in particular. "That isn't a gun, is it?"

Longarm was not paying attention at the moment, however, and did not bother to answer. His concentration remained on Herbert Hancock and Clementine Bonner.

The two of them seemed right determined to be the first one to spit out the answers that might help lead to a moderation of their eventual prison sentences.

At virtually the same moment they each spat out the name Longarm wanted. And then glared at each other in obvious fury.

Longarm ignored that too.

He motioned Hancock to move back away from the cane, then went forward and swiftly frisked the man for the second time that morning to make sure there were no weapons that he didn't know about.

When he was done with that he bent and retrieved the fallen malacca.

"That can't be . . ."

"Sure can," Longarm said. And after a moment he added with some satisfaction, "Not only can be, it is."

He turned and showed the others what he'd found.

The rubber tip of the cane slipped easily off to disclose the muzzle of a slender rifle barrel.

The heavy grip that was so cunningly shaped to look like a mallard-head grip for an ordinary walking stick was in fact a deceptively simple—and beautifully concealed—single-shot action. A twist and tug on the head cocked the mechanism and dropped a spring-loaded trigger into view. A pair of grooves cut as if by accidental scrape into the wood that sheathed the barrel would no doubt serve as rudimentary sights. Rudimentary, perhaps, but very effective in the hands of someone as thoroughly familiar with his weapon as Herbert Hancock obviously was.

"Well, I'll be a son of a bitch," Jesse whispered. Then he quickly added, "Beggin' your pardon, Miz Burdick."

"Jesse, I agree with you," she told him, "although I shouldn't put it in quite those words."

"Yes'm."

"How in the world did you figure that out, Marshal?" Howard Burdick wanted to know.

155

"Once I had this slug here in hand it wasn't all that hard. I mean, we all heard the shots. They were sharp and tinny. Sounded for all the world to all of us like a .22 pistol. Which it couldn't have been. I figured that much when I saw how far away the shooter was from me when he fired outside just a little while ago. I never heard of anybody that could shoot that good with a .22 pistol. Then when I got hold of this little slug an' took a good look at it—well, see for yourself." He handed it to George, who looked it over, nodded, and passed it on to the next man.

"The thing is flattened out some but the back end is intact. That isn't no .22. I'd guess a .32, prob'ly a rimfire like they chamber those little Smiths and the Ivor Johnson breaktops and some other revolvers for. This, o' course, is out of some gunsmith's custom shop. Only fires one round at a time, though, and can't be quick or easy to reload. By the way, Herbie, now that I think about it, you carry the spare cartridges in your tobacco pouch, don't you?"

"How did you deduce that?"

"It just come to me while we were talking here. When I looked you over this morning you had the pouch in your pocket. But no pipe that I recall, an' I haven't seen you smoke. So I figure that must be where you hide your ammunition for this ducky li'l shooting stick here."

Hancock sighed and tossed the pouch to Longarm. There was no tobacco in it. Just cotton wadding wrapped around a handful of loose .32 rimfire cartridges and four empty shell casings. Hancock was a careful assassin, and obviously hadn't wanted to point any fingers at himself by leaving unusual brass cases lying about.

"That was another thing I worked out after a spell," Longarm said. "We all swore we heard a .22 pistol. But then it occurred to me that the report from a short-barreled .22 would be about the same as the noise from a longer-barreled but slightly bigger-size cartridge. I never quite decided if I'd find a .32 or a .38, but I figured it pretty nigh had to be one or the other."

156

"Clever," Burdick said.

"Yeah, just cute as a basket full o' kittens," Longarm said dryly, looking square into Herbert Hancock's eyes while he did so.

"What now?" Burdick asked.

"Now we wait for the mud t' dry or the ground to freeze, an' I take my prisoners in for booking an' arraignment. After that it'll be up to the U.S. attorney what happens to them." He grunted and, again looking directly at Hancock first and then at Clementine Bonner, said, "If they don't give me trouble on the way back, that is. If they do, the United States government will pay the burial expenses. That's the decent thing t' do, after all."

He thought Hancock turned a mite pale at that. Clementine, of course, had already considered it. And come to her own conclusions.

"Herbie, old fellow, I got more cuffs with me, but they're all in my bag and that's atop Jesse's coach up the way a piece. D'you think I can trust you to stay put until I can get you safe in irons? Or would you rather take a chance on the alternative?"

"I can . . . be quite still, I assure you. You will get no trouble from me. No excuses."

"That's kinda a shame, Herbie. If you want t' change your mind, go ahead. Feel free." He smiled pleasantly— well, more or less—and lightly stroked the wooden grips on the butt of his .44 Colt.

"No trouble, Marshal. I promise."

Longarm took a seat where he could keep an eye on both prisoners, and accepted Mrs. Burdick's offer of coffee while he waited.

George, in the meantime, volunteered to go out to the stranded coach and bring Longarm's bag back so Hancock could be properly immobilized.

"Would you mind bringing the whole bag back, please, George?"

"Glad to."

Longarm nodded with considerable satisfaction. After all, Burdick's panatelas were not bad. But his own cheroots were better by far.

# Chapter 36

It was Saturday evening before Longarm, Jesse, and the shotgun messenger, George, walked out into the yard to stand with their heads raised and nostrils flared to the gathering breeze.

"What d'you think, Jesse? It's your call," Longarm said.

"Officially," Jesse agreed, turning his head and sending a stream of yellow-brown tobacco juice into the dark brown mud at their feet. "You tell us there's a man's life hangin' fire?"

"Yes."

"Six mules could die if I decide wrong and set out before the ground gets hard enough for us to make it through," Jesse added.

"That's true too," Longarm agreed.

"I do dote on my mules, Marshal. You know that."

"You treat them good as anybody I've ever known," Longarm said.

"But they ain't more important than a man," Jesse said, his voice rather sad at the thought.

"No, they aren't."

Jesse raised an eyebrow. "George?"

"I think it's gonna freeze tonight," George said. "You can smell it on the air. Almost like before a big snow comes

159

in. Though I don't look for a snow tonight. Too clear off to the west there. I say we got cold air moving in. Snow behind it, maybe, but by then we'd be well clear to the south.''

"You think we should try it, George?'' Jesse asked his shotgun guard. And friend.

"Yeah, I think we should try it. We won't ever have the stock any better rested than they are right now. And it was dried enough this afternoon already to get the coach in here, wasn't it? Well, I say it's dry enough we can get a start. Slow to begin with. We shouldn't put too much strain on the stock right off. Let them go slow and easy at first, till the cold comes on and the surface freezes over. After that we should have an easy roll the rest of the way down.''

"Marshal?''

"It isn't my place to say, Jesse.''

"But if it was?''

"Then you know I'd say we have to try it. That boy will die come dawn Monday if Mr. Overton and me can't find the proof of his innocence.''

Jesse sighed, and Longarm guessed he was thinking about his beloved mules.

"All right,'' the jehu finally said. "George, get the harness laid out ready while I pick the team. Marshal, would you be good enough to tell the passengers that we'll be rolling out of here in, say, forty minutes.''

"Glad to,'' Longarm told him.

"One thing more.''

"Yes?''

"If any of them want to stay over instead of risking the road like it is, the line will house and feed them free until the next southbound comes through. Or they can ride free back north when those boys decide to move.''

"All right.''

"And, um, I wouldn't want you to put pressure on anybody, Marshal. But I might mention to you that the lighter this coach the better for those of us who are in it. You know?''

Longarm smiled. ''I think the only people going south tonight, Jesse, will be the lawyer and me and my two prisoners. Somehow I don't think anyone else will want to ride out with us.''

''Yeah, well, whatever. I got nothing to do with any of that.''

''No, of course not.'' Longarm smiled and touched the brim of his Stetson before turning away and striding—it was dry enough now that he was wearing his own cavalry boots instead of the awkward gum rubber things Howard Burdick provided—back toward the relay station.

Saturday night, he kept thinking. Sunday morning into Bitter Creek. And that was if things went just right the whole rest of the way south. Then hit the rails and get off at Bosler. Then south—somehow; he had no idea how they would manage it—to the new diggings in the Medicine Bows.

After that . . . well, after that it would be like playing craps. With Gary Lee Bell's life as the wager lying on the come line.

# Chapter 37

If Bill Fay couldn't rightfully be considered one of Longarm's close friends, then the town marshal at Bosler could certainly be called a damn close acquaintance. The two peace officers had known each other the better part of two years or more, and had been known to share a bottle and to dispute a deck of cards. Longarm not only liked Fay, he trusted the local lawman. Which was more than he could say for a good many men in much more exalted positions.

Bosler was essentially a set of railroad loading chutes with a handful of houses and businesses growing up around them. It was also closer to the Medicine Bow gold diggings than the town of Medicine Bow, a few miles back up the line. That seeming anomaly was due to the fact that the minerals discovery was named for the mountains in which the ores were found, while the town of Medicine Bow was named for . . . God knows what; it wasn't anywhere close to the mountains of the same name. A stream, maybe. A legend. Or simply someone's idea of a joke. Longarm never had quite been sure.

Whatever the answer to that mild imponderable might be, Longarm was relieved enough when the eastbound Union Pacific coach finally squeaied and shook its way to a

alt at the Bosler platform at 1:32 p.m. on Sunday after-
oon.

"We'll get off here," Longarm told his traveling com-
anions. "If either of you wants t' run on ahead, feel free.
After all, this might be your lucky day."

Haycock eyed Longarm's Colt and seemed disinclined to
make a move that could in any way be interpreted as an
attempted breakaway. Clementine Bonner's veil kept Longarm from seeing where her attention lay. But he doubted
that the woman had any illusions about gaining her free-
om. Since the moment Longarm had gotten his carpetbag
back some days ago, her footsteps had been limited to a
maximum of nine inches per pace courtesy of a set of long-
chain manacles that he'd pressed into service as petite and
ladylike leg irons.

"Boy? You there."

"Yes, sir?"

"D'you know Marshal Fay, son?"

"Yes, sir."

"There's ten cents in it for you if you find him and tell
him Marshal Long needs his help."

"Marshal Long, you said?"

"That's right."

"Ten cents?"

"Uh-huh. The gentleman here will pay you ten . . . no,
make that twenty cents."

"Twenty?" The kid's eyes looked like they might cause
something to rupture if they got any bigger.

"What do you think, Tyler? Is twenty enough, or should
we—"

"Twenty cents, son," Overton confirmed before Longarm could run it up any higher.

After the swooning kid had raced away in search of Bill
Fay, the lawyer gave Longarm a look of feigned disgust,
then began to laugh. "Where did I come in on this deal?"

"Hell, everybody knows lawyers are rich, Tyler. You
can afford it."

163

"And the government can't?"

"Just trying to be a considerate public servant, Tyler, an' no squanderer of your tax dollars."

"Remind me to thank you sometime."

"I'll do that, Tyler." Longarm grinned. "Count on it."

The suddenly wealthy boy was back within minutes t report that Marshal Fay had been at Sunday dinner an would be along quick as he could get his boots and hat o

Overton gave the kid a two-bit piece and drew a raise eyebrow from Longarm. After the ecstatic boy disappeared the lawyer looked at Longarm and shrugged. "Don't loo at me like that. I didn't have twenty cents in smalle change. All right?"

"Hey, I believe you."

The kid had not been lying. Bill Fay turned up only minute or so behind the boy. The town marshal, who ha belly enough for several ordinary men, was wheezing an puffing but in good spirits.

"You look like you been running down fleeing felon: Bill," Longarm said as he pumped the fat man's hand.

"No felons around Bosler, Longarm. You know they'r all scared of my blinding speed."

"Yeah, I'd heard that about you. Bill, this is Tyler Ov erton from Talking Water up in Ross County. Careful wha you say where he can hear. He's a lawyer an' might tr an' hold you to your word."

"Howdy, Tyler. Any friend of Longarm here is a ma to not turn your back on. And all that kind of stuff."

"My pleasure," Overton responded.

"And what do we have here?" Bill Fay asked, eying th parties who were wearing steel.

"This lovely couple, that look like butter wouldn't me' in neither one of 'em's mouth, are a pair o' backshooter an' murderers, is what they are. These two you really bette not turn your back on. The woman there is the piano-wir garrote woman."

"My, oh, my. The one from Nebraska?"

"The very same."

Fay gave Clementine a positively luminous smile. "I've read so much about you, ma'am. Pleasure to see you in these, uh, circumstances. And the dandy gent?"

"Oh, he's a real special guest. Tried four times to kill me."

"Did he?" Fay asked with a straight face.

Longarm chuckled.

"Four times, huh? What's the matter, Longarm? Are you getting as slow as I am lately?"

"You'd think so, wouldn't you, me letting a little simp like him make four tries before I could catch him at it. Anyway, both of these will be facing federal charges before we give the states an' territories a crack at 'em."

"And judging from the fact that we are continuing to stand on a railroad platform instead of heading for the comforts of my jail, I take it you want to burden me with their care while you go off and play somewhere?" Fay guessed.

"Something on that order, Bill, yeah. I'll sign a voucher for you so you can bill the Justice Department for holding 'em."

"In that case, since there seems to be something in it for me, I will consider granting your petition for relief." He winked at Tyler. "Thought I'd throw a little legal-sounding language in there for you, Counselor. We like visitors to Bosler to feel at home while they're here."

Overton laughed.

"Seriously, Bill," Longarm said. "Don't trust neither of these two. They're cold killers, the both of them. Keep them locked down no matter how they complain. Me and Tyler won't be gone long. Don't take no chances with this pair until we get back."

"Mind if I ask where you're off to?"

Longarm explained where they were going. And why.

Fay looked Tyler over rather carefully for a moment, then asked, "I don't mean to imply anything personal, Mr. Overton, but how are you when it comes to fast horses?"

165

"Slow," the lawyer admitted. "But I fall off them pretty good."

"I kinda thought that might be so. Longarm, you know I'd never butt in where I don't belong . . ."

"Leopard changin' its spots, Bill?"

". . . but if you're interested, I just happen to have bought myself one hellfire fast team and buggy recently. Matched bays built like a pair of snakes with legs on them. Long skinny necks and hams no bigger than a decent housecat might have. They're ugly as sin, both of them. But fast? You'd best tie your hat in place and use a strong cord to do it. Best of all, they got stamina that you won't believe. They'll get you to the diggings before nightfall or else go ahead and kill them for trying. If they can't make the run that quick they're no use to me anyhow."

Longarm knew better than to believe that. Exactly. But he thoroughly appreciated the generosity that lay behind the statement.

"Damn, Bill, you keep on like this an' you're gonna make me feel bad about all the things I've said behind your back."

Marshal Fay threw his head back and roared. "Longarm, let me get these prisoners locked in nice and snug and then we'll put you fellows on the road south."

# Chapter 38

The team was as good as their owner claimed. Maybe better. It was still daylight when Longarm and Tyler Overton reached Chinaman's Knob. Still daylight, but barely. There was a pale salmon tint behind the imposing bulk of Medicine Bow Peak to the west, and beyond that lay the Sweetwater Basin and the Red Desert. Here, though, the country was wooded if not wet, and totally unlike the sere, dry plains below.

Chinaman's Knob was the latest in a succession of mining booms to bring mineral-crazed seekers of wealth flocking into the mountains.

It was said that a Chinaman had indeed made this latest discovery. It was also said that the Knob named in his honor was also the place where he was buried. After all, what right did some yellow-hued Celestial have when it came to staking out a minerals claim on good American soil.

All of that, however, was rumor, and Longarm had neither the time, the inclination, nor the authority to inquire into the truth that might be contained therein.

There was no public livery as such, but he located a feed sales barn with a smithy attached and a corral out back where the farrier's four-legged customers could wait to be accommodated. For a dollar and a half—in advance, courtesy of Mr. Overton—the smith agreed to grain, water, and house Bill Fay's team of bays.

"Strikes me as funny somebody would pay that much to take care of a pair as ugly as them things," the smith offered. After, it should be noted, he accepted the cash payment from Overton.

"You wouldn't have a team you'd like t' run against them, would you?" Longarm asked.

"You got to be kidding. Them? My grays would gag those bays with their dust." He pointed toward a set of stalls where a pair of obviously pampered grays with short, barrel-shaped bodies were munching bright hay.

"We got no time to make you a match, but the next time you get to Bosler you oughta look up Marshal Fay. These are his bays, an' I think he'd welcome a race. I hear he likes t' match his horses, but I don't think he does much against the teams over there. If you think your grays are good . . ."

The smith grinned, and Longarm guessed Bill would have himself a race in short order.

And in fact Longarm had not lied to the smith. Not a bit of it. The way he understood it, Bill no longer could do much against the competition in and around Bosler. Of course that was because his bays hadn't yet been beaten and at this point no one else was willing to take them on. Had Longarm neglected to make that clear to the Chinaman's Knob blacksmith? Gee, he thought it was all clear enough.

"Say, friend, you don't know a fella hereabouts name of Windy Williams, do you?"

"Williams? No, I don't recall anyone by that name. But then the camp isn't that old, and I wouldn't say I'm on close name-calling basis with more than a handful of fellas yet. I only been here myself a few weeks."

"The camp goes back to last year sometime, doesn't it?"

"That's what they tell me. But then it's all hearsay to me, don't you see."

"Sure, thanks. Uh, what's your recommendation for a place where a fellow might his whistle?"

The smith laughed. "Knock on any door you come to, mister. Likely it's a saloon. If it isn't, they'll pour you a drink anyway if you got cash money to pay for one."

"Chinaman's Knob not doing so well lately?"

"Let me put it this way. Since I got here most of my trade has been selling feed to fellas that want their stock strong enough to pull out for someplace else."

Longarm felt a sinking feeling. Even if Maddy's father was still alive and really had been spotted here in the Medicine Bows, there was a strong likelihood now that he might already have pulled up stakes and moved on to the next absolute, pure, and positively guaranteed bonanza of a gold strike.

"Thanks for your help, neighbor."

"Hell, thank you for the dollar and a half. It's a pleasure doing business with somebody that isn't dealing in promises. Damn thin, that promise soup."

"Yeah, I've had to eat a lot o' that my own self. We'll see you later. Oh, an' by the way. We might be needin' to pull out in the middle o' the night. If we do, we'd kinda appreciate it if you'd make sure who an' what is happening before you up and shoot at noises in the night. You know?"

"I'll keep that in mind."

Longarm waved a good-bye as he and Overton set out along the deeply rutted main, and only, street of Chinaman's Knob.

"Do you really think we have a chance to find Williams here?" the lawyer asked.

"Damn small," Longarm conceded. "But small chance is better than none, I reckon."

"And if we don't find him here, then what?"

"Then I expect we wire our regrets t' the widow."

"Jesus!" Overton said.

169

"Naw, no point in that. He'll already know."

"What?"

"Never mind."

"That looks like a saloon on that side of the street over there."

"Yes, and there's another just like it over here. Do you know Windy by sight?"

"Of course. He never employed my services, and I hadn't been in town very long before he disappeared. But Talking Water is a small community. I am sure I would recognize him if I were to see him again."

"Good. That means we can split up and go through these saloons separately. We'll cover them twice as fast."

"And if we don't find him?"

"Then we by God turn around an' go back through them all again. Just in case he's just come in or was in a back room with some whore the first time we looked. We don't have time to visit any other camp in these mountains, but this is the latest boomtown so we put our money down an' throw the dice right here, Tyler. This is our best shot, win or lose."

Overton nodded. "I'll take this side of the street. You take that one."

"I'll meet you at the other end."

# Chapter 39

Longarm groaned and squirmed about just a little. Something was tickling the right side of his neck. Unfortunately, it was not some pretty little thing doing it. He was sure of that much. After a few moments he came awake enough to identify the irritant. A wisp of hay that had invaded his shirt collar, and now was threatening to drive him plumb out of his mind.

He sat up, soft, sweet-smelling hay cascading to his waist from the loose blanket he had made of it, and began brushing himself off.

It was coming dawn. Time to wake up anyway.

With a yawn he stood and went over to the back door to take a piss.

Tyler Overton, he was surprised to see, was already awake and about. The lawyer was standing in the corral leaning on a rail and peering off toward the east.

There was not a damn thing out there worth looking at, and for a moment Longarm wondered what Overton was doing. Then he realized. He walked over to the man and stood beside him, putting an elbow on the cracking aspen rail and joining him in staring sightlessly toward the east.

"I'm sorry, Tyler. For whatever it's worth we did all we could."

"I suppose we did. But what was that you told the smith about promise soup being so thin? So is cream of regret, Long. Not only thin, it's bitter as hell."

Some hundred or more miles to the east in Cheyenne Gary Lee Bell should be mounting the hangman's scaffold just about this same time, Longarm figured.

Thirteen steps to reach the platform. That was what tradition said, whether it was true or not.

Flanked by the county sheriff on one side—or in this case some designated representative to stand in his place since the Ross County sheriff was back in McCarthy Falls—and a priest or preacher, whichever the prisoner desired, on the other.

Time enough for a few last, hopeless words if he wanted to waste the breath on them.

Then the hood.

Then the noose, its lumpy thirteen-twist knot placed just precisely so behind the ear.

And finally the wooden clunk as down below a lever was pulled by the state's official hangman. Who, Longarm happened to know, did *not* wear some bogeyman black costume, but a very neat and businesslike bowler and natty suit.

Longarm wondered what the last sound to reach the prisoner might be. The thump of the platform dropping?

More likely the sound of his own neck snapping as the bulk of the big knot pushed the spine sideways and caused the vertebrae to separate.

It was said to be a quick and painless death.

But who the hell could say that for sure? Nobody who ever went through it was able to tell about it after.

Whatever, it was a bitch of a way to die.

But then, hell, what wouldn't be?

Longarm sighed. The sun had made its first appearance over the distant horizon now, and was lifting free of the earth.

Official sunrise.

Madelyn Williams Bell should be a widow by now.

Shit! Longarm thought.

"Tyler."

"Mm?"

"Reckon we should hitch up the bays an' head back to Bosler now?"

"Yes, I suppose so. I . . . if you don't mind, Longarm, I'll ride along with you as far as Cheyenne. Someone will have to make arrangements on Maddy's behalf. I didn't . . . I never asked what she wants done now. I mean . . ."

"Take him home to her, Tyler. That's what I'd think."

"Yes, I suppose that would be best."

To give credit where it was due, Longarm thought, the defeated lawyer seemed genuinely saddened this morning. No man was that good an actor.

They went back inside, and were in the process of getting the harness sorted out ready to hitch the bay team to Bill Fay's buggy when Longarm heard the creak of rusty hinges as one half of the big double doors at the front of the feed barn swung open.

"Custis? Are you in there, Custis Long?"

"Who . . . ?"

A graying and withered but broadly grinning old man stepped inside and cheerfully proclaimed, "Somebody told me you was in town and looking for me, Custis. By Godfrey, it's good to see you again after . . . what's it been? Two years? Closer to three?"

Longarm gaped, taken completely aback.

Then his complexion turned a mottled, purplish hue and he barked, "You son of a bitch. You lousy, Judas son of a bitch!"

"Windy?" Tyler Overton exclaimed half a heartbeat behind Longarm's outburst. "Windy Williams. Jesus!"

173

# Chapter 40

Marshal Bill Fay came out of the Bosler town jail and waddled onto the street, his first concern being to see to the welfare of the fast bay horses and the hell with Custis Long and company. Once assured that his babies were unharmed, he was willing to greet Longarm and Overton.

"And who's the whiskery gent wearing the handcuffs?" the local lawman asked. "Not another murderer surely."

"Might as well be," Longarm explained sourly. "The sonuvabitch damn sure caused the death of another. Though not in any way the law can touch him for. Not that I can see."

"Then why the handcuffs?" Fay asked.

"Jeez, Bill, there's gotta be *some*thing we can charge him with. Not that me and Tyler have figured out just exactly what yet. But we'll think o' something. Count on it."

"Uh-huh. Kind of looks like in the meantime he's taken a fall and bruised himself up some. What did he do, fall down five or six times in a row?"

"Yeah, well, some people have lousy balance, don't they?"

Fay helped Williams down onto the street, and was compassionate enough to stand between the old man and Longarm. "I take it you didn't have any trouble finding him?"

174

"Hell, he found us. But not until past dawn this morning. He knew what was happening, damn him. Did it deliberately, he did. He was living there under a false name, and when he was sure Gary Bell was cold meat on the hook, then he stepped out all grins an' playful. Miserable old son of a bitch."

"Do you think he planned it all from the beginning?"

"The trial an' the hanging an' everything? Oh, hell, no. He couldn't have seen all that ahead. No, what I think— no point in asking him 'cause he'd lie like the sonuvabitch he is—what I think is that he just took off one day. The old fart never has been one to accept responsibilities. Things start t' pile up an' he heads for the other side o' the hill. But I think he didn't like Gary Bell none. I know he wouldn't care about Bell screwing his daughter. But I think he resented it when the hired man up an' married the girl an' took her away from her papa. Windy liked the way it was before, I think. Had all the advantages of Maddy being there to fetch an' do for him, but none o' the responsibilities of having a wife. I think he liked having a daughter better than he would've a wife. So when Gary Bell married her an' took her away from him, Windy didn't like it. An' when they decided up there that Windy was dead an' Gary Lee Bell killed him, the old bastard curled up an' hid on purpose instead o' stepping in to save the life of his own grandkid's daddy. That's low. You know?"

"It is low," Bill Fay agreed. "But it isn't fatal."

"Huh?"

"I did something yesterday that I hope you won't be mad at me for."

"What's that?"

"After you left here, Longarm, I kind of got to thinking. I knew my team would get you to the diggings by sundown, but after that it would take a pure-antee miracle for you to get back here in time to make it to Cheyenne before dawn. Even if you saw this man here the minute you pulled into town, that would've been hard because the last scheduled

175

eastbound last night went through at 10:12 p.m. No way you could have gotten back by then. Maybe if the team was fresh-rested for the run, but not on a turnaround. So what I did, Longarm, was to send out a telegram to the governor. It went out yesterday afternoon. I got a wire back earlier this morning.''

''What was—''

''The message I sent, I have to admit, I signed with your name. After all, who the hell am I to butt into other folks's jurisdiction. On the other hand, I added an endorsement under my own name. The governor and me go back a long ways, you see.''

''And you said . . . ?''

''What I told him was that there was strong evidence Gary Bell wasn't guilty and that I—meaning you, of course—would be along in a day or two to prove it one way or the other. If anyone ever asks, you didn't ask for a stay, just for a short postponement.''

''And this morning?''

''You and Mister Overton and this . . . person here . . . have until Friday morning to present yourselves before the appropriate authorities in Cheyenne. With or without your proof.'' Marshal Fay was grinning ear to ear.

''Shit, Bill. I owe you one. I owe you? Man, Gary Lee Bell owes you. I'll be sure an' tell him and his widow so.''

Longarm looked at Windy Williams, then back at Bill Fay. ''Let me ask you your best judgment on a legal opinion, Marshal. Me and Tyler have been arguing about it all the way back here from Chinaman's Knob.''

''What's that, Longarm?''

''If a man has already been declared dead by a duly seated territorial court o' law, Marshal Fay, can there be a charge placed against a man for killing that previously dead son of a useless bitch?''

''I think I'll have to take that under advisement, Longarm.''

''You do that, Bill.'' Longarm turned to Tyler. ''While

176

me and Bill here take care o' this bag of sour shit, whyn't you . . .''

"Send a wire telling them we're coming. Right. I'm already on the way." Overton headed for the railroad depot and telegraph office with a spritely spring in his step.

"All's well and all that shit, right?" Fay said.

"It remains t' be seen what's well and what ain't. Those kids ain't exactly outa the woods yet. Maddy's father turns out to be a true sonuvabitch, which won't exactly set well in the years to come, I'm sure. And the woman, who ain't a widow after all, still has t' tell her husband that she's pregnant even though he's been in jail a helluva lot longer than she's been knocked up. No, I wouldn't exactly say that everything is turning out peaches here, Bill." Longarm shrugged and reached for a cheroot. "On the other hand, Gary Bell is alive and is gonna stay that way. They got a chance to make it now. An' I suppose that's all any of us can ask for. Life don't come with guarantees. If we're given a chance, then I reckon we're doing pretty good."

"Come on inside, Longarm. We'll deposit your prisoner with the rest of the garbage you brought with you, then we'll go to lunch. There's time enough before the next eastbound is due in."

Longarm took Williams by the elbow and dragged him along like he would have led a dog on a leash. And not a particularly well-liked dog at that.

"I don't s'pose that same little ol' yellow-haired girl is waiting tables at the cafe beside the . . . where was that anyhow?" he was asking as they walked. "Was that in the block by the bank or . . .''

# Chapter 41

Longarm was tired. Lordy, but he was. Still, he was not ready to go home. Not quite yet.

He had left Tyler Overton and a very unhappy Windy Williams in Cheyenne, then made the long swing out to Julesburg on the U.P. and then back to Denver. He would be damned glad when the much-talked-about direct line from Denver to Cheyenne was completed. If it ever was.

He had to admit, though, that it was nevertheless better to ride a railroad coach than a stagecoach, so the longer route was better than a direct road without the rails.

Back in Denver he went through the formalities of booking Herbert Hancock and Clementine Bonner into custody awaiting arraignment—he figured he could follow up on that with the U.S. attorney tomorrow—and now wanted to complete the business he'd started, without ever knowing it, some days back.

"Yes, sir? Is there something I can do for you?" The desk clerk gave him a priggish, better'n-you look down the length of his delicately patrician nose.

Longarm could understand the reaction, he supposed. After all, he hadn't taken time to shave in, what, two days now. Something like that. No doubt he looked and possibly even smelled more or less like hell.

He could understand the reaction. That did not mean he approved of it. Or was willing to take it. Not in the mood he was in at the moment.

With a completely neutral expression he reached inside his coat and laid his wallet open on the counter to expose his badge, only slightly misshapen by the bullet that had struck it back at Burdick's station.

"First think you can do, bub, is change your attitude an' get real helpful. Otherwise I will personally drag your prissy ass down to the city jail and dump you in with the drunks and the crazies. An' if you think I won't do it . . ."

"Yes, uh, ahem, is there, um, is there anything I can do for you? Sir?"

"As a matter o' fact there is. Is Lord Matthew Welpole still in residence?"

"Yes, sir, he is."

"You can inform his lordship that his presence is requested in the ballroom."

"The Crystal Room is not open at the moment, sir. Might I suggest . . ."

"What you can suggest, shit-for-brains, is that the Englishman get his butt downstairs an' meet me in the ballroom. Which I believe just got open. Right?"

"Uh, yes, sir. As you say, sir."

The hotel clerk scurried in one direction while a glowering Longarm strode the opposite way.

It was at least a half hour before the ballroom door was opened and Lord Matthew Welpole came in, accompanied by a pair of rather competent-looking gents wearing side arms like they knew what to do with them.

"I don't believe I've had the pleasure," his lordship said.

"It pleased you well enough t' hire a gunman to take me down," Longarm said.

"Did I?" The Englishman seemed not at all perturbed by the accusation.

Longarm paused. And smiled at him. "You figure because I'm standing here your boy Hancock has t' be dead?

Wrong, old chap. Did I say that right? Old chap? Old chip
Which is it?''

"Chap, actually." It actually sounded more like "ek-
chually," but Longarm could make out what he meant.

"Right. Chap. Should be chip, I'd think. Like in buffalo
chip.''

"I beg your pardon?''

"Don't bother. What I was saying is that I think you are
a piece o' shit.''

"Is this your means of expressing friendly banter?''

"Not hardly. Y'see, I brought Hancock back alive. Him
an' his girlfriend both. It's really kinda funny to see the
two of them try an' be first to spill their guts, both of 'em
hoping for a deal with the prosecutors if they help put you
in the bag. The charge, by the way, is conspiracy t' assault
a federal officer. We'll start with that and see what else we
can work up to afterward.''

"You cannot possibly be serious.''

"Serious enough t' place you under arrest, you squat-t'-
pee cocksucker.''

Longarm wasn't sure, but he thought the lord might be
suffering an attack of apoplexy. Or something. Well, if the
man wanted to drop dead, Longarm supposed he could live
with it. He could think of worse things that might happen
than that.

"I cannot believe that . . . that . . . that . . . Milton, John
. . . you know your duty. Protect me.''

"Protect you, old chap? I ain't real sure this is sort o'
protection these boys signed on for.'' He smiled. "How
'bout it, Milt? John? Is that what you're paid for? Even if
you win, you lose. I shoot you today or the law hangs you
in a month or two. There's something t' look forward to.''

"Sorry, your lordship'' said one of them. "He's right.
He's a deputy U.S. marshal. You know what that means?
We can't drag iron on him.''

"Besides," the other one put in, "this particular lawman
is the one they call Longarm. I seen him shoot once. I'm

180

good, mister. But I'm not that good. I'm out of this one."

"So am I, your lordship. Sorry."

"Damn you both for cowards. Milton, give me your gun. Hand it over, if you please."

"I can't do that, your lordship. Sorry."

"At once, damn you. I insist."

"No, sir." The bodyguard backed away, hands held wide of his body so Longarm would not misunderstand his intentions. On the other side of the handsome Englishman the other bodyguard was moving aside as well.

Welpole was turned half away from Longarm now, reaching out toward the bodyguard called Milton.

That was not the hand Longarm was paying attention to, though. It was the one that was now hidden from his view that was of concern at this point.

It came as no great surprise, then, when the Englishman turned back to face Longarm. With a stout-barreled Webley in his fist.

Longarm almost regretted what he had to do. Almost, that is, but not in a big way.

The Brit had had his chance to give himself up, and if he wanted now to respond with a revolver . . . it was his choice.

Longarm's Colt appeared in his fist with the speed of a magician's sleight of hand.

The .44 roared, the sound of it shattering in the closed confinement of a room even the size of the hotel ballroom.

The two bodyguards, obviously no strangers to quick mayhem, pushed their hands high into the air and stood stone still.

Lord Matthew Welpole was still also, but only for a few lingering moments.

Then he collapsed. Very slowly, first sagging slightly at the knees, and then the torso doubling forward. Finally he dropped to the floor, the unfired Webley beneath his body.

A bright scarlet pool began to form under him and to spread across the shiny parquet flooring.

"Guess I won't arrest him after all," Longarm said.

"We weren't . . . I mean . . ."

"It's all right. You're both out of it. You made that clear enough."

"Yeah."

"Tell you what you can do now, if you would."

"Yes?"

"Whyn't you go tell Dame Edith she'll have to find a new game to play. She finally lost this one."

"Lost? Marshal, I guess you don't understand."

"How's that, Milton?"

"Maybe it isn't my place to say anything, but I been with the party since they came ashore in New York. And a person hears things, you know? Kind of puts things together sometimes?"

"Yes?"

"That woman upstairs, Marshal. She just won the game she was playing."

"How does that figure?"

"She inherits, Marshal. Everything that poor bastard had is hers now."

Longarm felt like the bodyguard had just kicked him in the stomach. Or worse.

Milton and the other guard turned and left the Crystal Room, leaving Longarm alone with a dead man. And with his own thoughts.

Dame Edith Fullerton-Welpole, Edy the high-kicking showgirl, won the final deal of the game.

And there was not a single damn thing Custis Long could do about it.

Slowly, wearily, he reloaded the one fired chamber in his Colt and shoved the revolver back into his holster.

What had he told Bill Fay? There are no guarantees in life.

And what a pity that was, eh?

He turned and walked away, through the lobby and onto the street, ignoring the snotty desk clerk whose questions hammered at him.

182

Watch for

**LONGARM AND THE JOHN BULL FEUD**

199th novel in the bold LONGARM series
from Jove

*Coming in July!*